4996

Stefoff, Rebecca
Thomas Jefferson:
3rd president of the
United States

Thomas Jefferson

3rd President of the United States

This painting shows Thomas Jefferson as he is most often remembered and honored—not as the third President of the United States, but as the author of the Declaration of Independence, one of the world's most historic documents. (Library of Congress.)

Thomas Jefferson
3rd President of the United States

Rebecca Stefoff

 GARRETT EDUCATIONAL CORPORATION

Cover: *Official presidential portrait of Thomas Jefferson by Rembrandt Peale.* (Copyrighted by the White House Historical Association; photograph by the National Geographic Society.)

Copyright © 1988 by Garrett Educational Corporation

Manufactured in the United States of America

Edited and produced by Synthegraphics Corporation

Library of Congress Cataloging in Publication Data

Stefoff, Rebecca, 1951–
    Thomas Jefferson, 3rd President of the United States.

    (Presidents of the United States)
    Bibliography: p.
    Includes index.
    Summary: Traces the life of the Virginia politician, American diplomat, and United States president and examines the domestic and foreign issues dominating his career.
    1. Jefferson, Thomas, 1743–1826 – Juvenile literature. 2. Presidents – United States – Biography – Juvenile literature. [1. Jefferson, Thomas, 1743–1826. 2. Presidents] I. Title. II. Series.
E332.79.S73 1988 973.4'6'0924 [B] [92] 87-32818
ISBN 0-944483-07-0

Contents

Chronology for
Thomas Jefferson

1743	Born on April 13
1760	Enrolled at College of William and Mary
1767	Admitted to Virginia Bar
1768	Elected to Virginia's House of Burgesses
1772	Married Martha Wayles Skelton on January 1
1776	Wrote Declaration of Independence in Philadelphia
1776– 1779	Served in Virginia legislature
1779– 1781	Served as appointed governor of Virginia
1783– 1784	Was member of Continental Congress at Annapolis, Virginia
1785– 1789	Served as U.S. minister to France, helped negotiate trade treaties
1790– 1793	Under President George Washington, served as first secretary of state
1797– 1801	Served as Vice-President under President John Adams
1801– 1809	Served as President of the United States for two terms
1816– 1819	Founded and designed the University of Virginia
1826	Died on July 4

Chapter 1

The Great Declaration

In June of 1776, England's 13 colonies on the east coast of America were seething with activity. Many of the colonists had grown angry at England's oppressive treatment. And some of these angry colonists were now calling for greater freedom, or even for independence. Neighbors and families found themselves forced to choose sides – to be Tories, remaining loyal to the King of England, or to become patriots, taking their chances on the gamble for liberty.

By now, freedom from British oppression was no longer just a matter for talk in marketplaces and taverns. In Massachusetts, colonists and British soldiers had already exchanged gunfire at Lexington and Concord. Other battles had followed. Red-coated British troops were arriving on each ship from England to swell the English garrisons. British vessels patrolled the coast. The colonists, in turn, were ready to use their muskets for fighting instead of hunting. They had formed militias in every community, as well as a Continental Army. They held torchlight rallies and demonstrations for independence in city and village squares.

The winds of war were blowing across the colonies, from seaports to frontier farms, from Massachusetts Bay to Georgia. In the midst of all this tumult, a 34-year-old Virginian named Thomas Jefferson sat in a small, low-ceilinged room in a house at 7th and Market Streets in Philadelphia, in the Pennsylvania colony. Although he was a patriot, Jefferson did not march with the Continental Army. Rather, he was a warrior of words who won one of the greatest victories of the Revolutionary War with pen and paper.

For 17 days, Jefferson sat at his desk wrestling with words, hoping to capture all that he knew and believed about human liberty, as well as the thoughts and dreams of his countrymen. This was not an easy task. Often he sat lost in thought for an hour, or crossed out a phrase or a line over and over again, rewriting until he felt the wording was just right.

Outside, in the broad Philadelphia streets, the stream of strolling families and bustling workers was dotted with groups of soldiers and militiamen, muskets over their shoulders. War had come to the colonies. Suffering would doubtless follow, and the outcome was uncertain. But surely the prize of liberty was worth fighting for.

Finally, Jefferson put his quill pen inside the writing desk and latched the lid with a sigh. He was tired, and he knew that a long struggle lay ahead. The fate of the colonies would be determined in the coming months and years. Well, he had done his best to give the colonists something to rally around, and to tell the world what they were fighting for.

As Jefferson finished his task that early summer day, he did not know that he had written one of the world's most historic documents: the Declaration of Independence. Its stirring phrases would do more than fan the fires of liberty in the American colonies. They would ring down the generations to become part of the world's heritage. And for his thoughts and his carefully chosen words, Jefferson would be remembered as one of the world's great men.

Benjamin Henry Latrobe, an artist and architect who lived at the same time as Jefferson, captured the pride and firmness of the young patriot. Jefferson probably looked much like this during the American Revolution. (Library of Congress.)

BACKGROUND AND BOYHOOD

It is not known when the ancestors of the Jefferson family arrived in the New World. Thomas Jefferson was unable to trace his father's family back further than his grandfather, but he reported a family tradition that the family had come originally from Wales.

Thomas' father, Peter Jefferson, was a self-made man. Born in 1708, he acquired enough education to become a surveyor. He made a living marking out property boundary lines and drawing maps. He was also a shrewd and industrious businessman, and acquired enough money to purchase about 6,000 acres in Goochland County (later to become Albemarle County), a sparsely populated area of western Virginia.

It was here, on the banks of the Rivanna River, that Peter Jefferson built a plantation that he called Shadwell. But he still continued his surveying and mapmaking activities in the unexplored hills and valleys of the region – these skills were highly prized in a growing frontier community. One of his tasks was to help establish a definite border between Virginia and North Carolina; another was to make a thorough map of the entire Virginia colony.

Peter Jefferson also became prominent in local affairs: he was at various times a justice of the peace, a sheriff, a judge, a commander of the local militia (volunteer defense force), and a representative from his county to the Virginia House of Burgesses (the colony's governing council under the supervision of the English governor). In 1739, he married Jane Randolph. She was the daughter of Isham Randolph, who had brought his family from London to America when Jane was a child. The Randolph family, which traced its ancestry back to King David I of Scotland (1084–1153), was well-to-do and influential. Peter Jefferson's marriage to Jane brought him into the inner circle of important colonial families.

Shadwell and Tuckahoe

Thomas was born on April 13, 1743, at Shadwell. He had two older sisters. The family later included four younger sisters and a younger brother. In addition to these eight, Peter and Jane Jefferson had two children who died quite young—not an uncommon occurrence in the middle of the 18th century, when medicine offered little protection against such illnesses as measles, smallpox, and diphtheria.

Thomas spent his first two or three years at Shadwell. Then Jane Jefferson's brother, William Randolph, died. Because Peter Jefferson had promised to be the guardian of William's son, he decided to move his family to William's home, Tuckahoe, in eastern Virginia near Richmond. Years later, Thomas said that his earliest memory was of the 50-mile horseback ride from Shadwell to Tuckahoe, with one of the family slaves guiding the horse.

For the next seven years, Thomas lived at Tuckahoe. He grew into a tall, long-limbed boy, with freckles, sandy red hair, and brownish hazel eyes. He had large hands and feet, and was prone to awkwardness and a slouching posture all his life. But he also had a winning smile and a friendly, sociable attitude. He loved the outdoors with a passion inherited from his mapmaker father. One of Thomas' favorite pastimes was hiking or riding for hours through the forests and along the mountain slopes, hunting or just observing the scenery and the wildlife.

Early Education

Both of his parents wanted Thomas, as their oldest son, to have the best education they could provide. The Shadwell plantation had become quite profitable, turning out a sizable crop of slave-grown tobacco each year, so money was no problem. As a small child, Thomas had private tutors at Tuckahoe. Then, after the Jeffersons moved back to Shadwell when Thomas was nine, he was sent to live and study at a boarding school run by a Scottish clergyman, the Reverend William Douglas, in Northam, Virginia.

Here Thomas began his study of the classical languages (Greek and Latin) and of French. He did not distinguish himself as a student at the Reverend Douglas' school, although he did love to read. Douglas found his pupil inattentive and given to too much daydreaming. Thomas, in turn, disliked Douglas and looked forward eagerly to the three or four months he spent at Shadwell every summer.

There was always something exciting going on at the Jefferson plantation: canoeing in the river, hunting deer and turkey in the mountains, riding every day, or listening to Peter Jefferson's stories about places he had been and things he had seen on his surveying travels. And at some point during these years, Thomas developed a great love of music, probably with the encouragement of his mother. He began to play the violin and eventually became a skilled violinist.

The Man of the Family

The pleasant days at Shadwell came to an end when Thomas was 14. Peter Jefferson died that year, 1757, and Thomas suddenly found himself the head of a large family and a large plantation. A family friend stepped in to serve as guardian until the young man was old enough to manage the family's affairs. As for Thomas, his course was clear. His father had wanted him to continue his education, and his mother agreed. He, too, was eager to do so—but not at the Reverend Douglas' school.

Thomas then enrolled in a school run by James Maury, who, like Douglas and most other colonial schoolteachers, was a clergyman. Because Maury's school was located in Fredericksville, which was fairly close to Shadwell, Thomas could spend his weekends at home. He soon discovered, though, that he liked school so well that he did not miss his beloved Shadwell. Maury's school was nothing like Douglas'. Under Maury's guidance, Thomas began a joyous, lifelong journey of learning.

A man of considerable education, Maury was a respected and influential colonial teacher. Among his later pupils were James Madison and James Monroe, both of whom would become friends of Jefferson and eventually follow him as President. Maury encouraged all of his pupils to take an interest in every aspect of the world. He led them on hikes through the Blue Ridge Mountains, looking for fossils and studying geology and the other sciences, and he gave them time for the riding and hunting that they all enjoyed.

This wise teacher urged Thomas to make the most of his love for languages. Thomas then mastered Greek and Latin so thoroughly that he was able to read books and poems in their original languages. At the same time, he continued his study of French and learned a little Spanish and Italian. He developed a passionate interest in history and loved to browse through Maury's large library, reading volumes of history, political philosophy, and the classics of English literature. He also worked at his violin-playing and took dancing lessons for six months.

Years later, Thomas was to point to the two years he spent at Maury's school as among the happiest times of his life. Shortly before the end of his second year there, when he was 16, he wrote a letter to a friend complaining that the large number of visitors at home sometimes kept him from school. He also said in this letter that he was beginning to think of seeing something of the world outside Albemarle County. Thomas eventually wrote thousands of letters in his lifetime, but this is the oldest one known to exist today. In its serious tone, its devotion to learning, and its impatience to see and experience the world, it is the true voice of Thomas Jefferson.

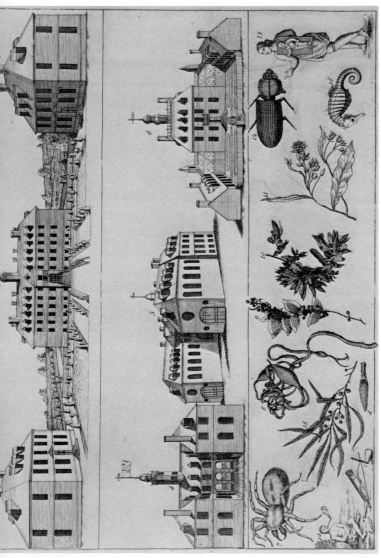

This old engraving shows some of the buildings associated with the College of William and Mary in Williamsburg, Virginia, as well as symbols of some of the subjects taught there. The creatures and plants represent natural history. The figures in the lower left and right corners are intended to represent Indians; they symbolize America. (Library of Congress.)

A WIDER WORLD

Later that year (1760), young Jefferson took his first step out into the wider world of which he had been dreaming. He entered the College of William and Mary in Williamsburg, Virginia. Both the city and the college offered him a host of new experiences.

Williamsburg was the grandest city in the Virginia colony. It had stately buildings, including the colony's white-pillared Capitol and the mansion of the British governor. It was a center of style and high society: elegant horse-drawn coaches, splendid silk and lace dreses for the ladies and knee breeches for the men, theaters, dances, and shops stocked with luxurious imported goods. For an unsophisticated 17-year-old, Williamsburg must have been tremendously exciting.

At first, college did not seem very exciting. The College of William and Mary was an unimpressive brick building, and Jefferson found himself far more advanced in his studies than most of his fellow students. Fortunately, however, he again met a gifted teacher who inspired and encouraged him. This teacher was Dr. William Small, of whom Jefferson later said, "He probably fixed the destinies of my life."

New Studies and New Friends

For two years, Small guided Jefferson's studies. He introduced his student to new disciplines: mathematics, literature, rhetoric (the art of using language effectively when speaking or writing), and natural history (a combination of biology and geology). Jefferson plunged into his courses with the enthusiasm he always brought to learning. He would read and study for as much as 15 hours a day, sometimes for weeks at a time. His restless, inquiring mind was never still.

At the same time, another chapter of Jefferson's life was beginning. He joined a social fraternity called the Flat Hat Club and became popular with the other students. One of his particular friends was John Tyler, who was later to be the father of the 10th President. Tyler and Jefferson, both violinists, joined a musical group and often practiced together. Another new friend was Frank Wills, a practical joker who sometimes hid Jefferson's books and overturned his desk.

Jefferson also made new and interesting friends outside the college, and through them he was drawn into thoughtful discussions of the colonies' economy and government. This new social and intellectual life was due to Dr. Small, who introduced his prize student to one of his own friends, George Wythe. A prominent and highly respected lawyer and scholar, Wythe later became the first professor of law in America. He, in turn, introduced Jefferson to Francis Fauquier, the lieutenant governor of Virginia, who was knowledgeable in economics and natural history.

Wythe and Fauquier, mature and important men, seem not to have minded that their new acquaintance was younger and less sophisticated. They respected Jefferson's intelligence and his curiosity, just as he admired their learning and experience. The three friends often met for dinner at the Raleigh Tavern, where they enjoyed a meal of venison stew and then sat for hours, sipping port wine and talking of art, science, government, and law. During these dinners, Jefferson recalled later, he heard "more good sense, more rational and philosophical conversation than in all my life besides."

TAKING UP THE LAW

During his two years at William and Mary, Jefferson began to think about his future. The plantation at Shadwell continued to be prosperous, and he knew that it could get by without

George Wythe, a prominent lawyer and scholar in colonial Virginia, befriended the student Jefferson and sparked his interest in law and politics. (Library of Congress.)

his constant attention. He was determined to be more than a well-educated gentleman farmer. His reading, together with his admiration of George Wythe, suggested to Jefferson that the law would be a worthy occupation. At about this time, too, Jefferson began to express an interest in social reform and politics, and he felt that a career in law might pave the way to activity in these areas. So, like many other aspiring young men in the colonies, Jefferson took up the study of law.

In colonial times, law students did not attend law school; instead, they learned by observing and helping a practicing lawyer. It was not uncommon for a successful lawyer to have two, three, or more apprentices or students working in his office. The apprentices read lawbooks and case records at the instruction of the lawyer. They also ran errands, did research, wrote legal papers and forms, and sometimes helped to present cases in court. In the process, they met other lawyers and influential citizens and had an opportunity to make a name for themselves as well as to learn their trade.

Jefferson apprenticed himself to his friend Wythe. He worked in Wythe's Williamsburg law office for five years, from 1762 to 1767. This was a somewhat long apprenticeship, but Jefferson had much to keep him busy. He spent a fair amount of time at Shadwell, visiting his family and seeing to the business of the plantation. He also read voluminously, and his studies included works that most other lawyers had not read: a dry, multi-volume collection of all the laws of England, for example, and Lord Kames' history of law. During his five years of study, Jefferson began to build his own library, in which philosophical, legal, and historical works outnumbered other books. His apprenticeship was also enlivened by his first serious affair of the heart.

A One-Sided Romance

In 1762 Jefferson met a young Williamsburg woman named Rebecca Burwell. Before long, he had fallen in love with her and began to think about marriage. He was 19; she was 16 — not unusual ages to plan to marry in colonial times. But he was a student who had just embarked on his legal studies and could not expect to take a wife until he had begun his own law practice. In addition, he had dreams of touring Europe after completing his studies. He hoped that Rebecca, who

John Marshall, who served as Chief Justice of the U.S. Supreme Court during Jefferson's presidency and for many years afterward, was the son-in-law of Jefferson's first love, Rebecca Burwell. (Library of Congress.)

seemed to return his affection, would agree to wait a few years for him.

One night in October of 1763, Jefferson and Rebecca attended a fancy ball at the Raleigh Tavern. Jefferson decided that the time had come to tell "Belinda" (it was the fashion of the time for young people to give romantic nicknames from myths or poems to their sweethearts) how he felt. Sadly, the young man who had already shown his skill with pen and paper made a rather poor showing of his first direct declaration of love. He confessed to a friend later that he had been able to manage only "a few broken sentences, uttered in great disorder, and interrupted with pauses of uncommon length."

Rebecca's affection for Jefferson apparently was not as strong as he had hoped. Before long, she was engaged to marry one of his friends, Jacquelin Ambler. Rebecca and Ambler had two daughters, one of whom later married John Marshall, who fought in the Revolutionary War and later served for many years as Chief Justice of the U.S. Supreme Court.

Chapter 2

Rumors of Rebellion

Throughout the colonies, the 1760s were a time of gradually growing unrest and unhappiness with British rule. In 1763, after nine years of fighting along the Canadian and American frontiers, the French and Indian War came to an end with England victorious against the French and their Indian allies. Victory was not cheap, however. England had war debts and decided to pay for them by taxing the colonies.

At this time, most people in the colonies did not think of themselves as Americans. They were English, Scottish, Welsh, or Irish in origin and thought of themselves as part of England under the rule of King George III. Those who could afford imported luxuries prided themselves on china, fine furniture, and fashions from England. British laws, customs, and manners prevailed everywhere without being questioned.

Then came the Stamp Act of 1765. This act was passed by the British Parliament to raise money from the colonies to help pay the debts incurred by the French and Indian War. It required the colonists to pay to have an official stamp, or

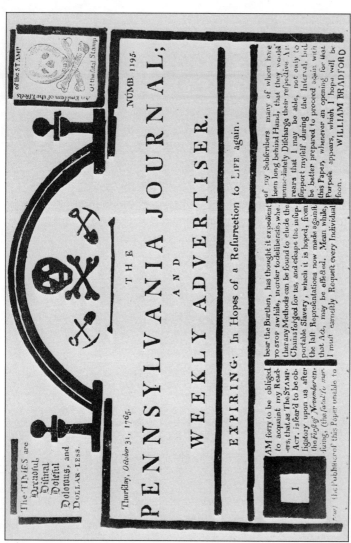

The Stamp Act of 1765 imposed strict taxes on many documents of daily life, even newspapers. The Pennsylvania Journal and Weekly Advertiser announces a suspension of its services during the "insupportable slavery" of the act. The skull-and-crossbones in the upper right corner is a parody of the stamp itself. (Library of Congress.)

seal, put on every important document: land titles, wills, contracts—even newspapers. Many colonists considered the Stamp Act outrageous and unfair, particularly because Parliament had imposed it without even bothering to consult the opinions of the colonists.

Suddenly the colonists became aware that they were ruled at long distance by a government on a tiny island far across the Atlantic Ocean, and that their taxes went to enrich a government in which they had no voice. Some of the colonists began to speak up, and what they said became a rallying cry: "No taxation without representation." Those who echoed that cry felt that the colonies deserved to have representatives in Parliament to protect their interests and to make the colonies an active part of the British government.

THE FIREBRAND OF VIRGINIA

One of the loudest and most eloquent voices raised in the colonies against the Stamp Act was that of Patrick Henry. He was a Virginian and a member of the House of Burgesses, to which Jefferson's father had belonged. One of the first colonists to speak out against British rule, Henry was a gifted and passionate speaker with the power to inspire his listeners. Jefferson had met him on a number of occasions and was impressed with his speech-making skill, especially because Jefferson now recognized that his own skill was in writing, not speaking.

Patrick Henry has sometimes been called a firebrand—that is, someone who starts a fire or inflames other people. The spark with which Henry started his fires was words. On a memorable day in 1765, soon after the Stamp Act had been

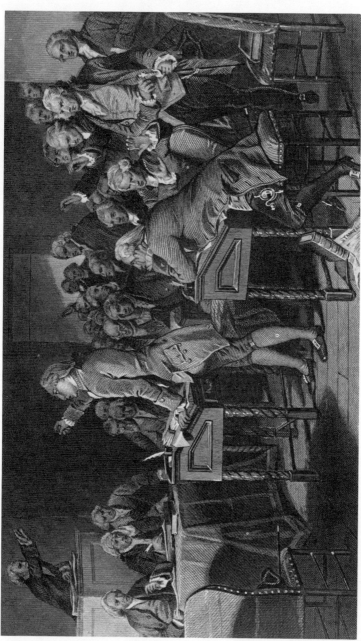

As his listeners erupt in a tumult of shouts, Virginian Patrick Henry (standing, center) calls for colonial independence in the Virginia legislature. He challenged his hecklers, "if this be treason, make the most of it!" (Library of Congress.)

Patriotic Patrick Henry

Patrick Henry, the firebrand of the American Revolution, was born on May 29, 1736, in Hanover County, Virginia. As a young man, he tried storekeeping and farming but failed at both. Because he had something of a reputation as a quick and lively speaker, he then decided to try for a career in law. Henry was admitted to the Virginia bar in 1760 and, within a few years, had a thriving practice. He became famous for his success in criminal cases, where his speeches were triumphs of wit and emotion.

In 1763, Henry won wide public notice from his eloquent speeches in the trial known as the Parson's Cause. Virginia had passed a law allowing farmers to pay clergymen in cash, rather than in tobacco as required by British law. The British refused to allow the law to stand. Henry's brilliant defense of the law revealed his opposition to British rule of the colonies. Over the next decade, he emerged as a leader of the anti-British movement, and he represented Virginia at the Continental Congresses of 1774 and 1775.

Unlike the colonists who felt that the colonies could remain linked to England under more lenient terms, Henry felt from the start that America was meant to be free and independent. He was convinced that independence could not be won except by war, and he argued in favor of creating an armed militia in Virginia. On March 23, 1775, in St. John's Church in Richmond, he urged the Virginia revolutionary convention to enter the war against England. The stirring conclusion of his speech is one of the most famous sentences ever uttered: "I know not what course others may take, but as for me, give me liberty or give me death."

During and after the revolution that he helped start, Henry served at various times as commander of the Virginia militia, as a member of the state's constitutional convention, as governor from 1777 to 1779, and as a member of the state legislature from 1780 to 1784 and again from 1787 to 1790. Family responsibilities and his own poor health caused him to turn down a number of offers of high-ranking positions in the new United States government.

In 1799, however, Henry agreed to run once more for the Virginia state legislature. As part of his campaign, he made his last public speech. It was a plea for the states to forget their differences in favor of long-lasting national unity. Henry won the election, but did not live to take his seat in the legislature. His fires were finally quenched when he died at home in June of 1799, at the age of 63.

proclaimed, Jefferson was in the audience of the House of Burgesses when Henry made an historic speech. To the amazement of his listeners, he claimed that the colonies had the right not only to be represented in Parliament but also to make their own laws, independent of England. A loud mur-

mur of astonishment rose from the spectators at this daring statement. But Henry went on to stir them still further.

"Caesar had his Brutus, Charles the First his Cromwell," he thundered, naming monarchs and the men who had assassinated them, "and George the Third . . ."

"Treason! Treason!" The hall erupted into a shouting match as loud cries interrupted Henry's speech. "Treason!"

. . . and George the Third," Henry roared above the tumult, "may profit by their example. If *this* be treason," he concluded, with a contemptuous glance at his hecklers, "make the most of it!"

Dazzled by Henry's eloquence and fervor, Jefferson returned to his rooms to ponder — not for the first time — the question of the colonies' rights. Like many other young people during the 1760s, Jefferson had felt the stirrings of dissatisfaction with British rule. He shared the exciting sense that change was possible, that great events were just over the horizon. And he had the advantage of a broad education to help him weigh the colonies' situation on philosophical, legal, moral, and historical grounds. Thomas began to feel that the practice of law might take second place in his interests to the challenges of political life. Before he could hope to make a mark in politics, however, his first task must be to complete his law apprenticeship and secure his place in the community.

A Lawyer at Last

Jefferson's apprenticeship to Wythe was completed early in 1767. In April, he passed the examination that admitted him to the Virginia bar (qualified him, that is, to practice law in Virginia). Later that year, the British Parliament passed the Townshend Acts, which ordered new taxes for the colonies on such goods as tea, ink, paper, and glass.

Amid the renewed outburst of political protest and controversy that the Townshend Acts provoked in the colonies, Jefferson began his new career as a lawyer and a justice of the peace. Like many colonial lawyers, especially those just starting out, he did not practice in an office but rather rode a circuit, representing clients and settling small cases in towns and villages throughout his district. The circuit-riding arrangement suited Jefferson's taste for riding and travel, and it gave him plenty of chances to spend time at Shadwell. Yet he began to grow impatient to get involved in public affairs. Before long, he would have his chance.

Chapter 3

Revolutionary Politics

For a year or two after passing his bar examination, Jefferson spent most of his time riding the circuit, accompanied by his slave Jupiter. The majority of the cases he dealt with involved land claims and property rights. Although he was not an inspiring courtroom orator like Patrick Henry, Jefferson prepared his legal papers and case presentations with careful thoroughness. Before long he began to make a name for himself as an up-and-coming lawyer.

On his circuit travels, Jefferson met people in all walks of life, and he gained first-hand knowledge of the activities and attitudes of Virginians. As a friend of Wythe and Fauquier, he was welcomed and befriended by prominent and influential people throughout the colony. Jefferson's intelligence and diligence were so impressive that, in December of 1768, he was elected to the House of Burgesses, following in his father's footsteps.

Jefferson took his seat in the legislature in early 1769. He was one of two members representing Albemarle County, and he was full of excitement at being part of his colony's political life at this crucial time. At 26, he was one of the youngest Virginians ever to serve in the legislature. For the next six years, his life would be a busy mixture of legal circuit-riding throughout the colony, personal milestones at Shadwell, and revolutionary politics in Williamsburg.

CHANGES AT HOME

The Jefferson family lost its home at Shadwell to a fire in February of 1770. The family and slaves escaped the blaze, but the house burned to the ground. Jefferson's first library—almost all of his papers and books—was destroyed. Undismayed, however, Jefferson then launched a project he had been planning for three years before the fire.

Jefferson's Little Mountain

In his will, Peter Jefferson had left to Thomas a plot of about 1,000 acres of land across the Rivanna River from Shadwell. It was a beautiful spot—a high, round hill overlooking the panorama of river, wooded valleys, neat farms, the city of Charlottesville, and banks of rolling hills that grew blue in the distance. Jefferson called this piece of land Monticello, which means "little mountain" in Italian. He loved it and wanted to build a home of his own on it.

At the time, the notion of building an estate on a hilltop was considered absurd. Rivers were the most-used avenues of transportation in the colonies, especially for plantations, which shipped out their cargoes of cotton, tobacco, and other goods by boat. Most Virginia estates were built in valley bottoms, close to the river docks. But Jefferson was full of new ideas. He wanted his home to have the benefit of the magnificent hilltop view, and he wanted to design it himself.

Several years before, an elderly cabinet-maker (as furniture-makers were called then) had given Jefferson a book about architecture. With typical confidence and enthusiasm,

Jefferson studied the book and immediately began drawing plans for his own home. He dreamed of creating a small but elegant mansion, fronted with white pillars and surrounded by gardens and orchards. Now, after the fire at Shadwell, it was time to begin construction.

By November of 1770, one part of the building had been completed, so Jefferson moved into Monticello, his new estate. He wrote to a friend that the finished structure was really only a single room that must serve as parlor, kitchen, hall, bedchamber, and study until the rest of the construction was completed.

Although Jefferson had hoped to build Monticello in a year or two, it was nearly a decade before the primary construction was done. In truth, however, Monticello was never really finished. For the rest of his life, Jefferson would ceaselessly add to, change, and remodel his home on the hill. But its graceful, simple beauty was apparent from the start. With no architectural training except what he had picked up from reading a book, Jefferson had designed and built one of the finest structures of his or any other time.

A New Romance

"Many and great are the comforts of a single state," Jefferson had written to a friend after the failure of his courtship of Rebecca Burwell. He often spoke of his determination not to get married. But he was a personable, interesting man—more than six feet tall, with wavy, tousled hair and broad shoulders, who could dance, play the violin, and talk entertainingly and intelligently on just about any topic. In addition, he owned a large plantation, was doing well in his profession, and—as a member of the House of Burgesses—was a man of some importance. Many women found him attractive, and he could not deny his interest in some of them.

Monticello, Jefferson's "little mountain" home, was one of his finest creations. He designed it all himself, with only enthusiasm, energy, and an old architecture book to guide him. Today it is a museum and public monument, and much of it looks just as it did in Jefferson's time. (Library of Congress.)

None of them attracted him seriously, though, until he met Martha Wayles Skelton in Williamsburg in 1770.

Martha Skelton was a pretty young widow. No portraits of her have survived, but she is said to have had auburn hair and hazel eyes, like Jefferson's own. She was charming, well educated, and an experienced household manager in spite of her youth—she was only 22 when she and Jefferson met. Her first husband, whom she had married at age 18, had died in 1768, leaving her with a baby son. She also possessed a large estate, although it was crippled with heavy debts.

Jefferson's interest in Martha Skelton was returned. She loved music as much as he did, and during their courtship they often played duets, he on the violin and she on the harpsichord (a small, piano-like instrument). Legend says that one day another man who was also courting Martha came to call on her at her father's house. Standing outside the house, he overheard the melodious sound of one of her duets with Jefferson. When he heard how beautifully the two played and sang together, he gave up in despair and went home without announcing his presence.

A Snowy Honeymoon

This time around, Jefferson's courtship went smoothly, and his proposal of marriage was accepted. The wedding took place on New Year's Day, January 1, 1772, at The Forest, as the home of Martha's father in Charles City County was called. The newlyweds spent several weeks at The Forest, but Jefferson was impatient to take his bride to the uncompleted mansion at Monticello, 100 miles away.

The Jeffersons set off from The Forest for Monticello in the middle of one of the most severe snowstorms in the history of Virginia. The roads were covered with deep, soft snow, and their carriage finally bogged down in the drifts several miles from their destination. They then had to finish the journey on horseback.

Upon arriving at Monticello, the Jeffersons set up housekeeping in their one-room brick home. The first of their six children was born the following September. She was named Martha, for her mother, but she was soon given the nickname "Patsy." Although she was small and frail as an infant, Patsy gained strength and developed into a healthy child, with much of her father's energy and vigor.

Not all of the Jefferson children were so lucky. Only two, Patsy and her younger sister Mary, called "Polly," lived to adulthood. Three other daughters and a son died in infancy or early childhood. Jefferson's stepson, Martha's child by her first husband, died in May of 1773.

Despite the sadness of the children's deaths, Jefferson had much to make him happy in the early 1770s. He was the proud owner of Monticello, which kept him busy with plans and construction. He was devoted to his wife and daughter, and they to him. He had an estate to manage and a law practice to tend. Most absorbing of all, he was finally getting involved in the world of politics. Like George Washington of

Virginia, Benjamin Franklin of Pennsylvania, John Adams of Massachusetts, and others throughout the colonies, Jefferson was swept up in the tempestuous events leading to the American Revolution.

MOVING TOWARD WAR

Ever since the hated Stamp Act of 1765 and the Townshend Acts of 1767, opposition to British rule had been growing in the colonies. Jefferson believed that England's administration of the colonies—an administration that consisted mostly of heavy taxation—amounted to no more than tyranny. While many colonists hoped that the American colonies would continue to be governed by England under improved laws and with representatives in Parliament, Jefferson went further. He felt that the American colonies must become independent. If they were to be associated with England by ties of trade and diplomacy, it should be a relationship of two equal sovereign states, not of one state and its colonies.

Taxes and Boycotts

After taking his seat in the House of Burgesses, Jefferson soon became known as one of the leaders of the anti-British movement. He was one of a group of officials who voted in 1769 to pass a resolution that said that the people of Virginia, not the British Parliament, should impose taxes on Virginians. England reacted quickly and decisively by dissolving the House of Burgesses. The angry members then called an emergency meeting in the Apollo Room of the Raleigh Tavern.

This was the same room in which Jefferson had tried and failed to propose to Rebecca Burwell years before. Now, however, he had no time to waste thinking about the past.

He and the other representatives knew that they had to do something to keep from being crushed by England's taxes. They made a solemn pledge to boycott (that is, refuse to buy) any goods that were taxed by British law. Groups in the other colonies soon did the same. As hard as it was to live without tea, glass, newspapers, and other staples of daily life, the colonists knew that the boycott would hurt the tradesmen and merchants of England more than it would hurt them. The greatest danger of the boycott for the colonists was that it was an unmistakable act of rebellion. What would England do?

To the great relief of the colonists, England gave in and repealed (cancelled) all of the taxes except the one on tea. But the repeal did not restore peace and good feeling; it brought only an uneasy calm, like the calm before a great storm. The colonists still resented the tax on tea. Even more, they resented the fact that England could simply ignore or overturn the colonists' own forms of government.

Before the French and Indian War, the colonists had been left pretty much alone to govern themselves. They developed a variety of methods for self-government, ranging from the town meetings of New England communities to Virginia's House of Burgesses. But now that England seemed determined to mine the wealth of the American colonies through taxation, the privilege of self-government was being taken away from the colonists. Quite a few of them did not intend to stand for it.

Committees of Correspondence

In the early 1770s, people who shared anti-British feelings formed Committees of Correspondence in every colony. These committees were something like underground newsletters. They kept each colony informed of activities in all the other colonies, and they gave individuals from widely separated regions a chance to get to know one another and to exchange views through the mail. Before long, members of the committees were calling themselves patriots; colonists who remained loyal to England, however, called them rebels.

Jefferson was a member of one of the first Committees of Correspondence. Always at his best with pen and paper, he argued forcefully in his letters for the colonists' right to govern themselves independently. These letters were circulated among such other patriots as John Adams, his cousin Samuel Adams of Boston, and Ben Franklin. The readers formed a high opinion of the young Virginian's ideas — and of his writing ability. A few years later, this recognition of Jefferson's skill as a writer would have important consequences.

A Massacre and a Tea Party

In the wake of demonstrations against the Stamp Act and the Townshend Acts, further hostility between the colonists and the British seemed inevitable. One memorable clash occurred in Boston in March of 1770, about the time Jefferson was breaking ground for Monticello's first building. A crowd of protesters in Boston taunted a group of British soldiers into firing upon them; in the following riot, three colonists were killed.

The patriots seized upon this sad event and called it the "Boston Massacre," hoping to suggest that the British had fired upon innocent civilians for no reason. The story of the massacre made good propaganda, and feelings ran high against the British throughout the colonies when the news spread. One patriot who did not want the episode to be distorted for propaganda purposes was John Adams of Massachusetts; he courageously acted as lawyer in the defense of the soldiers, claiming that they deserved as fair a trial as anyone else.

A few years later, a second incident, also in Boston, brought the outbreak of war nearer still. Boston was a major seaport, and in December of 1773 three British merchant ships were moored in its harbor. Those ships carried tea — tea that would be sold to the colonists only if they paid the hated tax on it. The colonists didn't want to pay the tax, but they did want to send an unmistakable message to the British. So a group of patriots formed a daring plan.

On the night of December 16, 150 men, probably led by Samuel Adams and rather unconvincingly disguised as Mohawk Indians, crept along the harbor jetties, boarded the three British merchantmen, and dumped 342 chests of costly tea into the icy waters of Boston harbor. The colonists cheered this brave gesture, which they called the "Boston Tea Party," but the British government was not amused.

Feeling that it must act swiftly and firmly to protect its rights and the rights of British property-owners, Parliament ordered Boston harbor closed to all shipping until the British East India Company was repaid for its lost tea. It also imposed severe restrictions on citizens' rights in the Massachusetts Bay colony. These punitive restrictions, which were referred to by the unhappy colonists as the "Intolerable Acts," brought relations between the colonies and England close to the breaking point.

THE CONTINENTAL CONGRESSES

The Virginia House of Burgesses, which had started calling itself the Virginia Assembly at the time of the boycott in 1769, received word of the Intolerable Acts in the spring of 1774. A group of the most patriotic members, led by Patrick Henry and another lawyer named Richard Henry Lee, decided that it was time for the colonies to take action together.

This drawing from 1846 shows colonists cheering while patriots disguised as Indians throw chests of tea from British ships to protest the tax on tea. The Boston Tea Party, as this event of 1773 came to be called, brought the colonies close to war with England. (Library of Congress.)

The members of this small group, which included Thomas Jefferson, met in a back room of the Raleigh Tavern and wrote a revolutionary proposal. They claimed that England's oppression of the Massachusetts colonists was really an attack against the people of all the colonies and should be resisted by all the colonies. They suggested that each colony's Committee of Correspondence should send delegates to a central meeting, which was to be called a "Continental Congress." The purpose of this Continental Congress would be to organize a unified resistance to England.

The idea of a Continental Congress was a revolutionary one for two reasons. The first was the notion that the colonies should act together as a united force. Ever since the beginning of settlement in the New World, the colonies had experienced rivalry and friction among themselves. People were accustomed to thinking of themselves as "Rhode Islanders" or "North Carolinians." Only a few visionary thinkers like Jefferson and Franklin had arrived at the idea of "Americans."

The second revolutionary element was, of course, having a meeting, without the permission of the British government, to plot against British interests. Those who spoke out in favor of such a meeting were certain to encounter the displeasure of the British authorities, at the very least. Nevertheless, the First Continental Congress was scheduled for September of 1774. It was to meet in Philadelphia, the colonies' largest city and the center of artistic, cultural, and social life.

A Dangerous Subject

Jefferson was not selected to be a delegate to the First Continental Congress. He was, however, assigned a task of considerable importance. He was asked to write a document for the delegates setting forth the arguments in favor of reduced taxation. But Jefferson went far beyond the limits of the job he was asked to do. When Virginians met in Williamsburg in August of 1774 to choose their delegates to the Continental Congress, they read Jefferson's lengthy essay with surprise and some concern. He called it *A Summary View of the Rights of British America,* and it did much more than argue against taxation.

In *A Summary View,* Jefferson maintained that the colonies had no obligation to remain under England's control. He claimed that, in leaving England for America, the colonists had broken their old ties with the parent country and had actually founded a new state. Now, he went on, the colonists had the right to form a society and a government of their own.

A Summary View did not speak out in favor of violent revolution against England. However, it did state very clearly that Parliament had no authority in the colonies and that the colonists' continued association with the King of England would be voluntary, not mandatory.

Very few colonists, even the most patriotic, were ready to go quite that far. George Wythe, Jefferson's old friend and teacher, felt that his former apprentice's position was too extreme. So did George Washington, the influential planter and patriot. Most felt that they should avoid the issue of independence and try instead to get England to give the colonists the same rights as other English citizens: representation in Parliament and local self-government. So the Virginia delegation did not officially adopt Jefferson's statement of position. But *A Summary View* was published in Williamsburg, Philadelphia, and London. It earned for its author the reputation of a gifted writer and a committed revolutionary. After the pamphlet was published in England, the British government put Jefferson's name on its list of "dangerous subjects." He was in distinguished company. The list already included Patrick Henry, John Adams, and Samuel Adams.

First Continental Congress

Twelve colonies sent delegates to the Continental Congress of 1774–1775; only Georgia stayed away. The Congress was headed by Peyton Randolph of Virginia. It passed resolutions condemning British taxes, continuing the boycott against British goods, and approving the creation of armed militias in the colonies. In Massachusetts, colonists who foresaw the coming of war were already amassing stockpiles of weapons and ammunition and drilling in militia regiments.

In Virginia, Jefferson was present when Patrick Henry called for the immediate formation of a militia for the colony. "War is inevitable!" cried the firebrand in a speech in Richmond. "And let it come!" It came all too soon. A month later, on April 19, 1775, the first shot of the Revolutionary War—"the shot heard 'round the world," as it was later called by poet Ralph Waldo Emerson—was fired at Concord, Massachusetts.

Now, in the birth pangs of a new nation, families and communities were torn apart by conflicting loyalties. It was a time of pain, uncertainty, and confusion for many people in the colonies. It was also, for Jefferson and other patriots, an intensely vivid and exciting time.

Second Continental Congress

Jefferson was appointed a delegate to the Second Continental Congress, which met in Philadelphia in May of 1775. This time Georgia was present. Jefferson, at age 33, was one of the youngest members of the Congress, but his intelligence and abilities made their usual good impression on the older and more experienced men around him. John Adams said of Jefferson that he was "so prompt, frank, explicit and decisive upon committees and in conversation . . . that he soon seized my heart."

Before long, Jefferson was given plenty of work to do. When news reached Philadelphia that the Britsh Parliament had just passed a law prohibiting the colonies from trading with any country other than England, the Congress erupted in an outraged uproar. Now even the most moderate delegates recognized that they could not keep peace with England.

The Battle of Bunker Hill soon followed. Then the Congress appointed George Washington, who had fought well in the French and Indian War, as the commander-in-chief of the newly formed Continental Army. Jefferson wrote to his Martha of these events that "war is now heartily entered into."

Jefferson himself was busy at what he did best: writing. He was asked to prepare a document that would explain why the colonies had taken up arms against England. He called his production *Declaration of the Cause and Necessity for Taking Up Arms* and submitted it to his fellow delegates for review. Like *A Summary View,* it was judged to be too extreme and belligerent. John Dickinson, a delegate from Pennsylvania who was known to be very moderate, was asked to tone it down a bit. Even after Dickinson's changes, however, the document accused England of oppressive and tyrannical behavior. It also called for independence, saying that the colonists were determined "to die Freemen rather than to live Slaves."

Return to Monticello

In August of 1775, Jefferson took a short break from the Congress to visit his family at Monticello. Sadly, his infant daughter died soon after his arrival there, and both his wife and his mother were very ill. He returned to Philadelphia to take up his duties in September, but he was worried and fearful about what might be happening at home. "The suspense under which I am is too terrible to be endured," he wrote to his brother-in-law. "If anything has happened, for God's sake let me know it."

At the end of December, Jefferson received word that his wife and his mother were failing fast. He left the Congress as quickly as he could. When he arrived at Monticello, he found Martha recovering but his mother extremely unwell. He stayed at home during her final illness; she died several months later. He did not return to Philadelphia until May of 1776. When he did, he found a new task awaiting him.

THE DECLARATION OF INDEPENDENCE

On June 7, 1776, Richard Henry Lee of Virginia proposed a resolution to the Congress: "That these United Colonies are, and of right ought to be, free and independent States, that they are absolved from all allegiance to the British Crown, and that all political connection between them and the State of Britain is, and ought to be, totally dissolved." This was the point of no return. If the Congress accepted the resolution, there could be no possibility of compromise with England. The war would continue until the colonies had won their liberty—or until the revolt had been crushed.

The delegates decided to postpone the vote on Lee's resolution. In the meantime, five delegates were asked to form a committee to prepare a statement of the case for independence. The five were John Adams, Benjamin Franklin, Robert R. Livingston of New York, Roger Sherman of Connecticut, and Jefferson. Because Jefferson was known to be an excellent writer and a champion of independence, and because he represented the large and influential Virginia colony, the others agreed to leave the job to him. He returned to his quarters on Market Street, opened his mahogany writing desk, and took up his pen. Seventeen days later, he emerged with the Declaration of Independence.

When he sat down to write, Jefferson said many years later, his goal was "not to find new principles, or new arguments, never before thought of, not merely to say things which had never been said before; but to place before mankind the common sense of the subject, in terms so plain and firm as to command their assent, and to justify ourselves in that independent stand we are compelled to take . . . and to give that expression the proper tone and spirit called for by the occasion." He succeeded. The Declaration of Independence did not set forth any new and unheard-of principles. Rather, it drew upon familiar political arguments; it appealed to the emotions of the stirred-up colonists; and it used the language of the law courts, churches, and all educated people of Jefferson's time. But it is universal in its application. In attempting to explain why 13 small colonies on the eastern edge of the North American continent deserved independence, Jefferson created a defense of liberty for all nations and all peoples with the following words:

When in the course of human events, it becomes necessary for one people to dissolve the political bonds which have connected them with another, and to assume among the Powers of the earth, the separate and equal station to which the Laws of Nature and of Nature's God entitle them, a decent respect to the opinions of mankind requires that they should declare the causes which impel them to the separation.

We hold these truths to be self-evident, that all men are created equal, that they are endowed by their Creator with certain unalienable rights, that among these are Life, Liberty, and the pursuit of Happiness.

That to secure these rights, Governments are instituted among Men, deriving their just powers from the consent of the governed.

That whenever any Form of Government becomes destructive of these ends, it is the Right of the People to alter or to abolish it, and to institute a new Government, laying its foundations upon such principles and organizing its powers in such form, as to them shall seem most likely to effect their Safety and Happiness. Prudence, indeed, will dictate that Governments long established should not be changed for light and transient causes; and accordingly all experience hath shown, that mankind are more disposed to suffer, while evils are sufferable, than to right themselves by abolishing the forms to which they are accustomed. But when a long train of abuses and usurpations, pursuing invariably the same Object, evinces a design to reduce them under absolute Despotism, it is their right, it is their duty, to throw off such Government, and to provide new Guards for their future security.

Such has been the patient sufferance of these Colonies; and such now is the necessity which constrains them to alter their former Systems of Government. The history of the present King of Great Britain is a history of repeated injuries and usurpations, all having in direct object the establishment of an absolute Tyranny over these States. To prove this, let Facts be submitted to a candid world.

He has refused his Assent to Laws, the most wholesome and necessary for the public good.

He has forbidden his Governors to pass Laws of immediate and pressing importance, unless suspended in their operation until his Assent shall be obtained; and when so suspended, he has utterly neglected to attend to them.

He has refused to pass other Laws for the accommodation of large districts of people, unless those people would relinquish the right of Representation in the Legislature, a right estimable to them and formidable to tyrants only.

He has called together legislative bodies at places unusual, uncomfortable, and distant from the depository of their public Records, for the sole purpose of fatiguing them into compliance with his measures.

He has dissolved Representative Houses repeatedly, for opposing with manly firmness his invasions on the rights of the people.

He has refused for a long time, after such dissolutions, to cause others to be elected; whereby the Legislative powers, incapable of Annihilation, have returned to the People at large for their exercise; the State remaining in the mean time exposed to all the dangers of invasion from without, and convulsions within.

He has endeavoured to prevent the population of these States; for that purpose obstructing the Laws of Naturalization of Foreigners; refusing to pass others to encourage their migrations hither, and raising the conditions of new Appropriations of Lands.

He has obstructed the Administration of Justice, by refusing his Assent to Laws for establishing Judiciary powers.

He has made Judges dependent on his Will alone, for the tenure of their offices, and the amount and payment of their salaries.

He has erected a multitude of New Offices, and sent hither swarms of Officers to harass our People, and eat out their substance.

He has kept among us, in times of peace, Standing Armies without the Consent of our legislatures.

He has affected to render the Military independent of and superior to the Civil power.

He has combined with others to subject us to a jurisdiction foreign to our constitution, and unacknowledged by our laws; giving his Assent to their Acts of pretended Legislation:

For quartering large bodies of armed troops among us:

For protecting them, by a mock Trial, from Punishment for any Murders which they should commit on the Inhabitants of these States:

For cutting off our Trade with all parts of the world:

For imposing Taxes on us without our Consent:

For depriving us in many cases, of the benefits of Trial by Jury:

For transporting us beyond Seas to be tried for pretended offences:

For abolishing the free System of English Laws in a neighbouring Province, establishing therein an Arbitrary government, and enlarging its Boundaries so as to render it at once an example and fit instrument for introducing the same absolute rule into these Colonies:

For taking away our Charters, abolishing our most valuable Laws, and altering fundamentally the Forms of our Governments:

For suspending our own Legislatures, and declaring themselves invested with power to legislate for us in all cases whatsoever.

He has abdicated the Government here, by declaring us out of his Protection and waging War against us.

He has plundered our seas, ravaged our Coasts, burnt out towns, and destroyed the Lives of our people.

He is at this time transporting large armies of foreign mercenaries to compleat the works of death, desolation and tyranny, already begun with circumstances of Cruelty & perfidy scarcely paralleled in the most barbarous ages, and totally unworthy the Head of a civilized nation.

He has constrained our fellow Citizens taken Captive on the high Seas to bear Arms against their Country, to become the executioners of their friends and Brethren, or to fall themselves by their Hands.

He has excited domestic insurrections amongst us, and has endeavoured to bring on the inhabitants of our frontiers, the merciless Indian Savages, whose known rule of warfare, is an undistinguished destruction of all ages, sexes, and conditions.

In every stage of the Oppressions We have Petitioned for Redress in the most humble terms: Our repeated Petitions have been answered only by repeated injury. A Prince, whose character is thus marked by every act which may define a Tyrant, is unfit to be the ruler of a free people.

Nor have we been wanting in attention to our British brethren. We have warned them from time to time of attempts by their legislature to extend an unwarrantable jurisdiction over us. We have reminded them of the circumstances of our emigration and settlement here. We have appealed to their native justice and magnanimity, and we have conjured them by the ties of our common kindred to disavow these usurpations, which would inevitably interrupt our connections and correspondence. They too have been deaf to the voice of justice and of consanguinity. We must, therefore, acquiesce in the necessity, which denounces our Separation, and hold them, as we hold the rest of mankind, Enemies in War, in Peace Friends.

We, therefore, the Representatives of the United States of America, in General Congress, Assembled, appealing to the Supreme Judge of the world for the rectitude of our intentions, do, in the Name, and by Authority of the good People of the Colonies, solemnly publish and declare, That these United Colonies are, and of Right ought to be Free and Independent States; that they are Absolved from all Allegiance to the British Crown, and that all political connection between them and the State of Great Britain, is and ought to be totally dissolved; and that as Free and Independent States, they have full Power to levy War, conclude Peace, contract Alliances, establish Commerce, and to do all other Acts and Things which Independent States may of right do. And for the support of this Declaration, with a firm reliance on the Protection of Divine Providence, we mutually pledge to each other our Lives, our Fortunes and our sacred Honor.

Chapter 4

A Statesman at Home and Abroad

Jefferson completed his draft of the Declaration of Independence on June 28, 1776 — just in time. The other members of the Declaration Committee still had to read it and make their contributions, and the Congress was scheduled to vote on Richard Henry Lee's resolution calling for independence on July 2. The vote was held, and the resolution was passed. The war between the colonies and the British was no longer just a war against unfair taxes. It was now officially a revolution, a war of independence.

THE DECLARATION'S DEFENSE

The Congress' next order of business was to vote on Jefferson's Declaration. The document was presented to the assembly very much as its author had written it, with a few editorial changes and additions by Franklin and Adams. The author listened for two days while the various delegates examined the document he had crafted so painstakingly. They debated every line, every phrase.

Throughout these two days of debate, Jefferson remained silent, from either modesty or nervousness — most likely he felt both. The Declaration's staunchest defender was John Adams of Massachusetts. So vigorously did he support the Declaration of Independence against its critics in the Congress that Jefferson and others called him the "Atlas of Independence," after the Greek myth of Atlas, the giant who bears the weight of the world on his shoulders.

The delegates to the Congress made a few changes in Jefferson's draft. Most of them were matters of style, changes of a word here and there. The only significant change was the deletion of a paragraph that attacked King George III for allowing the slave trade to continue. The delegates from Georgia and South Carolina insisted that this section be removed. Because they came from states whose economies depended upon slave labor, they did not want the issue of slavery to become part of the question of independence.

Jefferson, Adams, and the others agreed to the changes. At last the document was accepted. Adams' eloquent speeches in defense of the Declaration moved the delegates to vote in favor of accepting it on the afternoon of July 4, 1776, the day that has come to be known as America's Independence Day.

The Declaration Goes Public

The very next day, a printer named John Dunlap delivered the first printed copies of the Declaration of Independence to the congressional delegates, who in turn began sending them to the legislatures of the various colonies. The document was read aloud to citizens everywhere — in market squares, in taverns, and in churches. Some of the listeners were shocked and alarmed by the seriousness of the situation. Others tossed their hats into the air and cheered with enthusiasm. After the Declaration was read to an excited crowd in New York City on July 9, the people cast ropes around a statue of King George III and toppled it from its pedestal.

Two weeks after the Second Continental Congress accepted the Declaration, the delegates ordered a formal parchment copy of the document to be drawn up for signing, which began on August 2, 1776. John Hancock of Massachusetts was the first to sign; 55 others eventually followed.

The act of signing the Declaration of Independence made the delegates traitors to England—a crime that was punishable by death. They were, of course, well aware of this fact, but they felt it was a risk that had to be taken. Said Benjamin Franklin as he stepped forward and took up the pen, "Now, gentlemen, we must all hang together, or assuredly we will all hang separately." To protect the lives of the signers, their identities were kept secret for almost a year.

Jefferson signed with the other Virginia delegates, after his friends George Wythe and Richard Henry Lee. Nothing in his signature or any other notation in the document identifies him as the author.

SERVING VIRGINIA

The acceptance and publication of the Declaration of Independence marked Jefferson's greatest contribution to the fight for freedom. It also marked, he felt, the end of his usefulness to the Continental Congress. He longed to be home at Monticello and back in the Virginia legislature, where a new constitution of the now-independent colony was being written and developed. Jefferson never stopped feeling that service to his native colony or state was as worthy and important as national service.

Several times during the summer of 1776 Jefferson requested permission of the Continental Congress to return to Virginia. The request was denied because the leaders of the Congress felt that he might be needed in Philadelphia. Frus-

trated at being left out of Virginia's constitutional deliberations, he drafted a constitution and sent it to Williamsburg.
But by the time it arrived, the state's constitution was largely
completed. In October, however, Jefferson was able to leave
Philadelphia. He then hurried to Virginia and took his seat
in the state legislature, where he set about at once working
to reform some of the old colonial laws and to put his own
ideas into practice.

New Laws for Landowners

By this time, Jefferson had developed some deeply thought-
out beliefs about the nature of a republican state. (A republican form of government is one in which citizens who are en-
titled to vote elect officials to govern them according to law.)
He seized the opportunity of his service in the legislature to
incorporate these beliefs in the new laws of Virginia. He
wanted, as he said, to eliminate laws that supported "ancient
or future aristocracy" and to create "a government truly
republican."

In other words, Jefferson believed that the American
Revolution gave the people of the former colonies a chance
not just to declare themselves independent of England but
to create a new and completely different kind of society. He
did not want the United States to become a country like England, with a privileged aristocratic class. Instead, he had
a vision of a nation of self-sufficient, independent small
farmers and landowners who had the ability to educate their
children and participate in their government. To make this
vision a reality, Jefferson worked hard in the state legislature
to encourage four important reforms in Virginia law.

The first change was the reform of the law of entail.
Based on traditional British laws of land inheritance, the en-

tail law allowed some land estates to remain in the control of single families for generations. An entailed estate could not be sold by its inheritors, even if they wanted to sell it. The system was designed to protect and preserve the large hereditary estates of the British aristocracy, and Jefferson felt that such a system had no place in republican America. He succeeded in his effort to have the law repealed.

Closely related to the entail law was the object of Jefferson's second attack, the law of primogeniture. Like entailment, primogeniture was a feature of British land law. From the Latin words for "first" and "offspring," primogeniture meant that land that was entailed could be inherited only by the oldest son of the landowner. In other words, the owner of an entailed estate could leave money and other property to all of his children, but only his oldest son could inherit any of the land. The law of primogeniture was designed to keep aristocratic estates from being divided among many children. Jefferson succeeded in abolishing this law, too.

Now all landowners could sell or divide their property in whatever way they wanted. This was a significant victory for Jefferson. He believed that land should be available to all who could afford to buy and work it, and should not be restricted to the private use of a privileged few for generations.

Freedom of Religion

The third of Jefferson's reforms concerned religion. The Church of England (also called the Anglican Church) had long been established as the official church of Virginia. It was wealthy and powerful, supported by taxes imposed upon all citizens—even those who did not follow the Anglican faith. Jefferson felt strongly that religion was one subject that must lie outside the scope of government. Therefore, he believed, government support or persecution of any religion was wrong.

Jefferson's own religious beliefs were considered daringly liberal by the standards of his time. Like most young Virginians, he had been brought up in the Anglican faith. From an early age, however, he claimed that he believed in God but not in any one organized religion or church. "I am a real Christian," he said, "that is, a disciple of the doctrines of Jesus." As an adult, Jefferson did not belong to any church. He did, however, attend services at various times in churches of all denominations, and he contributed money to churches that he thought were doing good works.

The key to Jefferson's religious thinking was that he did not care which religion was "right," or whether any of them were right. He only cared that the opinions of all people, whatever they might be, should be tolerated in a free state. Religion, to Jefferson, was an intensely personal business. An individual's religious beliefs should be no one else's concern—and certainly not the concern of the state. "It does me no injury for my neighbor to say that there are 20 gods, or no god," he said. "It neither picks my pocket nor breaks my leg."

He embodied this philosophy of religious toleration in the Virginia Statute of Religious Liberty, a bill which he hoped the legislature would pass. The bill declared that "no man shall be compelled to frequent or support any religious worship" and that "all men shall be free to profess, and by argument to maintain, their opinion in matters of religion."

To Jefferson's disappointment, the bill encountered opposition and delays in the legislature. Its chief enemy was the clergy, who prospered in a system of state-supported religion and compulsory church attendance. Finally, in 1786, after a decade-long battle, the Statute of Religious Liberty became law. By then, Jefferson had left the Virginia legislature, but he counted the passage of the statute as one of his great achievements.

Education for All

The fourth of Jefferson's major reforms involved education. As a lover of learning, he had come to believe that the people of a republic would need knowledge and reason in order to govern themselves well and preserve their liberty. "If a nation expects to be ignorant and free in a state of civilization," he wrote, "it expects what never was and never will be."

Jefferson argued that it was the responsibility of the state to provide education at all levels to all of its people. This was a completely new idea in an age when all schools were private and only the well-to-do could afford an education. Jefferson worked out a detailed plan for public education in Virginia. It included elementary schools across the state, grammar and classical schools in several locations, a free state library, and a college or university. Jefferson was ahead of his time in regard to education, however, and the plan was not accepted by the legislature. Eventually, Jefferson was able to achieve only one part of his broad plan for public education, but even that was delayed for many years.

In addition to his four reforms, Jefferson took part in other legislative business between 1776 and 1779. He was one of a group of legislators who wrote a new version of the state's code of crimes and punishments. The group wanted to eliminate the death penalty for all crimes except murder and treason and to make some of the other punishments less cruel and more humane. This revised penal code was finally adopted by the state in 1796. Jefferson also succeeded, in 1778, in getting a law passed that prevented any more slaves from being imported into Virginia.

The War Rages On

During these years, while Jefferson divided his time between his home at Monticello and the legislature, which was now established in the new state capital at Richmond, the Revolutionary War was being fought on the battlefields of the northern colonies. General George Washington crossed the Delaware River to attack the British in Trenton, New Jersey, in December of 1776. A year later, he and his army froze in their winter quarters at Valley Forge, Pennsylvania. The war dragged on. Jefferson and others cheered every American victory and grieved at the news of the Continental Army's defeats and suffering.

It was all very well, complained some of the revolutionists, for Jefferson to pen his eloquent call for liberty. But now that others were fighting and dying on the battlefield in defense of that liberty, Jefferson was home at Monticello, tending his gardens and reading his books. The story goes that once, before a battle in New Jersey, Washington called the roll of his aides and fellow officers and then asked sarcastically, "Where's Jefferson?"

In fact, Jefferson never felt himself qualified to be a soldier. He also believed that preparing for a new society and a new government after the war was just as important as the actual fighting. And, because lawmaking and writing were what he did best, he was satisfied to serve in those ways. But when the war moved south, Jefferson found himself in a new role—one that did not suit him so well.

GOVERNOR JEFFERSON

After several years of fighting, the British found that the rebellious Americans were putting up a stiff resistance in the North. So, under the command of Sir Henry Clinton, the British forces turned their attention to the South. In December of 1778, they captured Savannah, Georgia. Soon they were outside Charleston, South Carolina. In May of 1779, the war came to Jefferson's home state. A British fleet anchored off Hampton Roads and nearly 2,000 red-coated troops swarmed through Portsmouth, Virginia, burning farms and looting towns. The terrified Virginians knew that worse would soon follow.

One month later, the legislature appointed Jefferson governor. At this time, the governor of Virginia did not have strong executive powers. Instead, the governor's office was controlled by the Council of State, an eight-member committee elected by the state legislature. The governor had no veto power and little decision-making power—which is, perhaps, why Patrick Henry wanted to give up the job to Jefferson. The governor's chief responsibility was to organize the defense of the state against the coming British attacks. Unfortunately, Jefferson had no experience as a military commander and little to work with in the way of troops.

Because the Continental Army was far to the north, it could not reach Virginia for several months. In the meantime, the state was defended by militiamen, local volunteers who were poorly trained and even more poorly armed. Although they were supposed to join regiments at the call to battle, the Virginia militiamen were understandably afraid to leave their homes and families to the mercies of the British. Many of them deserted, and some even joined the British. Jefferson did his best to make plans, secure supplies for the troops, and keep his militia officers posted, but the British forces were far too superior. In dozens of skirmishes and battles, the Virginians were soundly defeated.

Benedict Arnold, an American brigadier general in the Revolu-
tionary War who had also fought bravely in the French and In-
dian War, joined the British army when he was not promoted to
major general. Since then, his name has been synonymous with
"traitor" for Americans. In January of 1781, Arnold led British
soldiers into Richmond, forcing Jefferson to flee to Charlottes-
ville. (Library of Congress.)

A Flight to the Hills

The hardest blow came in January of 1781, during Jefferson's second term as governor. An American general named Benedict Arnold, angry because he had not received a hoped-for promotion, turned traitor and joined the British army. Arnold led a detachment of British Redcoats into Richmond, which they set afire. Helpless to resist, the state government fled to Charlottesville. The incident brought much criticism of the poor defense of the capital.

Soon afterward, Jefferson's term of office expired. The legislature was ready to appoint him to another term, but he declined. He felt that his background and skills were not best suited to supervising military campaigns, and he asked to be relieved of further responsibility for governing the state. He then retired to Monticello before his successor to the governorship was named.

Upon arriving at his home, Jefferson received word that a British unit was advancing on Monticello, possibly to capture him. His capture would be an embarrassment to the Americans and a triumph for the British—for although he was no longer officially the governor, he was still the closest thing to a governor that Virginia had at the moment. Jefferson hurriedly bundled his wife and children off in a carriage and then fled on horseback, narrowly escaping capture by galloping along the back roads and mountain paths he had known all his life.

Like the evacuation of Richmond, this incident also provoked criticism. Some people claimed that Jefferson had been an incompetent leader in a crisis; others accused him of being cowardly. In the face of these accusations, the legislature appointed a special committee to investigate Jefferson's conduct. After the committee reported that the charges of incompetence and cowardice were unfounded, the legislature passed

The state capitol in Richmond was one of the colonies' most elegant buildings. Governor Jefferson ordered an evacuation of the capitol and other public buildings when British forces approached. Although he was later criticized for cowardice, a committee of investigation denied the charge. (Library of Congress.)

a resolution honoring Jefferson for his "ability, rectitude, and integrity" and thanking him for "impartial, upright, and attentive administration whilst in office."

Despite these words of praise from the legislature, his years as governor were not happy ones for Jefferson. The burning of Richmond had pained him deeply, and turning down the governorship at a time when the state desperately needed a leader had been a difficult decision. But Jefferson felt that he simply was not cut out to be a wartime leader, and he resolved to live with his decision, even though it hurt his popularity and cost him some political status. Soon, however, his mind was distracted from his political problems by other matters.

RETIREMENT AT MONTICELLO

Not long after Jefferson left office, the tide of the war turned in Virginia. The French, who had entered the war on the side of the Americans, sent a fleet commanded by Admiral Comte François de Grasse. Washington's Continental Army moved down from the North, as did American troops led by the French Marquis de Lafayette and the German Baron von Steuben. On October 19, 1781, these forces launched a major attack at Yorktown, Virginia, against British troops led by Lord Cornwallis. This decisive battle ended the long, bitter war. Cornwallis surrendered, and the American colonies were free. A peace treaty between England and the United States was signed in Paris two years later, in September of 1783.

Jefferson was at Monticello, to which he had retired after giving up the governor's office, when he received the happy news of the American victory at Yorktown. But because he was upset about the criticism he had received as governor, he claimed to have no more interest in public office. He said that nothing would ever separate him again from his farm, his family, and his books.

One good thing had come out of Jefferson's governorship, however. He had taken on a young man as a clerk and law student, and the two had become good friends. The young clerk was James Monroe, a Virginian who had served with distinction in the Continental Army during the early years of the war. Monroe liked and admired Jefferson, and often sought the older man's advice about his own career in law and politics. The relationship between the two men would span decades, during which both would serve as President of the United States.

For now, though, Jefferson abandoned thoughts of public life and carried on with the work that needed to be done at Monticello and his family's other farms: overseeing the planting, harvesting, building, and countless other tasks of a growing country estate. Jefferson also found time to begin work on a project that eventually became the only book he ever published.

The book, called *Notes on the State of Virginia,* was a detailed survey of the climate, geography, settlements, history, economy, society, and laws of Jefferson's native state. It revealed his remarkable gifts of observation and description and his fine scientific mind. But woven through this factual account were threads of original, philosophical thinking—about slavery, government, human nature, religion, and a variety of other topics of universal interest and importance. In *Notes on the State of Virginia,* Jefferson used his description of one state as an opportunity to reflect on the entire world and its people. It was a brilliant book on all counts, and it kept him busy for several years.

A Death in the Family

Jefferson's productive retirement was disrupted in 1782 by a great personal loss. His beloved wife, Martha, bore their sixth child, a daughter, in May. Weakened by childbirth, she fell ill. Throughout the summer and fall, Jefferson spent every waking moment either at her bedside or writing in a small alcove attached to her room. In spite of his devoted care, Martha Jefferson died on September 6.

Jefferson was desolated. "He fell into a state of insensibility from which it was feared he would not revive," his daughter Patsy later wrote. After Martha's funeral, he stayed in his room for three weeks. When he emerged, it was to take long, solitary horseback rides in the hills around Monticello. Patsy recalled that "he was incessantly on horseback, rambling about the mountain, on the least frequented roads, and just as often through the woods." Patsy sometimes accompanied her father on what she called "those melancholy rambles."

Only after several months of lonely sorrow did Jefferson begin to consider his future. At age 39, he was a widower with three daughters: Patsy, Polly, and Lucy Elizabeth, the youngest, who would die several years later. He was unhappy at Monticello, which was filled with memories of Martha, so he welcomed a summons to return to the political life he had given up a year earlier.

PHILADELPHIA AGAIN

The Continental Congress was now meeting in Philadelphia under the terms of the Articles of Confederation, a forerunner of the Constitution. No one was yet certain just what form of national government might emerge to link the 13 independent colonies, but the Congress strove to present a united front on such matters as trade agreements and the peace negotiations with England. John Adams and Benjamin Franklin were in France to discuss the terms of the peace treaty with British representatives, and in November of 1782 the Congress asked Jefferson to join Adams and Franklin.

Leaving his daughters in the care of trusted slaves, Jefferson hurried to Philadelphia, but found that the ship on which he was to sail to France was locked in the harbor ice and could not depart. The journey was delayed for several months, until word was received in Philadelphia that the treaty had been worked out and Jefferson's help would not be needed. In the meantime, the lively atmosphere of postwar Philadelphia restored some of Jefferson's interest in life. Before long, he was bustling about on congressional business. His spare time was spent in combing the bookshops for volumes and maps, and in animated conversations with his old comrades from the 1770s.

Congressman Jefferson

From early 1783 until May of 1784, Jefferson represented Virginia in the Continental Congress, which moved from Philadelphia to the nation's new temporary capital in Annapolis, Maryland. He made two contributions to the Congress during this period.

The first was to establish a decimal (based on units of ten) monetary system to be shared by all the states. Instead of continuing to use British pounds and shillings, or creating 13 separate systems of currency, the states would now share dollars, dimes, and other American coins.

The second of Jefferson's contributions involved the

Northwest Territories. This was the name that had been given to the huge tract of western land that later would become the states of Ohio, Indiana, Illinois, Michigan, and Wisconsin. Jefferson wrote a plan describing a system of administration for the territories and a method of allowing them to become states in a fair and orderly manner. Many of his recommendations were used in the Northwest Ordinance of 1787, a congressional act that became the formal plan for expansion into the Northwest Territories.

Jefferson's duties in Annapolis came to an end in May of 1784, when he was asked again by Congress to go to France. This time he was to help Adams and Franklin draw up trade agreements with France and other European nations. He accepted with pleasure and anticipation. More than 20 years after he had dreamed of asking Rebecca Burwell to wait until his return from a tour of Europe, Jefferson was finally going to cross the Atlantic.

VIVE LA FRANCE!

Jefferson sailed for France from Boston. Patsy, then 12 years old, accompanied her father; Polly remained in Virginia in the care of an aunt and the family slaves. Upon their arrival in Paris, Patsy was enrolled in the Abbaye Royale de Panthémont, a girls' school operated by the Catholic Church—but only after Jefferson had made sure that she would not receive religious instruction. Then Jefferson set out to discover what Paris had to offer.

He was delighted with the grand and elegant architecture of buildings like the Cathedral of Notre Dame and Versailles Palace. He spent hours browsing through rare, musty volumes in the open-air bookstalls that lined the banks of the River Seine. He feasted in wonderful restaurants and developed a taste for fine French wine, of which he eventually became a noted connoisseur and collector. And, true to his lifelong habit of careful observation and record-keeping, he took notes about the many things that interested him: statues, recipes, bird and plant life, and the customs and habits of the people.

Jefferson also worked diligently on the trade negotiations. In 1785, he was asked by Congress to replace the elderly Franklin as the official United States minister (ambassador) to France. For the next four years, he represented the United States at the French court and worked to build not just trade but friendship between the two countries.

Also in 1785, Jefferson's book, *Notes on the State of Virginia,* was published, first in France and then in the United States. It brought its author international recognition as a writer and thinker. When, in 1786, the Virginia Statute of Religious Liberty was passed into law, Jefferson's reputation as a champion of freedom grew still greater.

After Jefferson had been in France for several years, he sent for Polly, his younger daughter, who was then about nine years old. Accompanied by a slave named Sally Hemings, Polly sailed to England. There she was met and cared for by Abigail Adams, the wife of John Adams, who was then serving as United States minister to Great Britain.

Later, Polly joined her father in France. He enrolled her in the same school that Patsy attended. Shortly thereafter, Patsy astonished her father by telling him that she wanted to become a Catholic and was even thinking of becoming a nun. Jefferson promptly withdrew both girls from the convent school, after which they lived with him and studied with tutors for the duration of their stay in Paris.

The French Revolution

That stay ended in 1789, when the French Revolution broke out in Paris. Jefferson had long foreseen a class war between the oppressive French aristocracy and the suffering and poor masses of the common people. He was proud of the fact that one of the principal documents of the French Revolution, the Declaration of the Rights of Man, which had been written by his friend, the Marquis de Lafayette, was modeled on his own Declaration of Independence. Like many Americans, Jefferson believed that the American Revolution had inspired the French Revolution. He was prepared to view the French republicans as revolutionary brothers.

Nevertheless, he was appalled by the bloodthirsty and uncontrollable nature of the civil war that reigned in France, and he was not sorry to see his term as minister to that country come to an end. He wanted to return to the peaceful blue hills and quiet gardens of Monticello. What he returned to, however, was the chaos and confusion of a brand-new government.

Chapter 5
Party Politics

W hen Jefferson left for France in 1784, the 13 newly independent states were bound together in a loose association under a set of agreements called the Articles of Confederation. This confederation, or association of independent states, was not really an effective form of national government. It could not collect taxes, establish a nationwide military force, or form consistent trade and diplomatic relations with other nations.

Although there were some people who felt that the former colonies should continue to exist as 13 separate sovereign nations, most people recognized the need for some form of unified, national government. The small states, weakened and impoverished by the Revolutionary War, needed each other's support and cooperation to survive and flourish. And there were some essential functions, such as maintaining a military force and establishing treaties with other countries, that could most efficiently be done by a central government.

During Jefferson's years in France, two Americans led a movement aimed at forming a stable and secure national government. They were James Madison of Virginia, a close friend of Jefferson, and Alexander Hamilton, a brilliant young lawyer from New York. At their urging, the Continental Congress called a special convention in Philadelphia in 1787. Its purpose was to draft a constitution for the new federal, or national, government of the United States of America.

"WE THE PEOPLE. . . ."

Throughout the hot Philadelphia summer, 55 delegates to the Constitutional Convention discussed and debated a multitude of issues in the red-brick building that has come to be called Independence Hall. Madison later confided to Jefferson that getting the various interests and factions from the 13 states — merchants and farmers, shippers and plantation owners, northerners and southerners — to agree had been almost more difficult than beating the British. The Constitution that the convention adopted after several months of deliberations began with the historic words, "We the people of the United States, in order to form a more perfect Union. . . ." It established the United States government—"of the people, by the people, and for the people"— much as we know it today.

That government consisted of three branches: the executive, headed by an elected President; the legislative, composed of elected senators and representatives; and the judiciary, consisting of a court system topped by a Supreme Court. A system of checks and balances was used to prevent any part of the government from gaining too much power over the other two. The Constitution gave the federal government the ability to do what was needed for the new nation: raise money through taxation, negotiate treaties, and create a defense force.

The Bill of Rights

The Constitution prompted much debate. Some Americans, including Jefferson, were fearful that a strong central government would end up too much like the oppressive tyranny of England. Jefferson was particularly worried because the Constitution did not contain a clear statement of the rights of individual citizens. Nonetheless, he felt that the advantages of cooperation and unity among the states far outweighed the dangers that might occur if each state simply went its separate way, so he supported the Constitution. But he continued to argue for a statement of individual rights, and his friend Madison seconded his argument. These rights—including freedom of speech and freedom of religion—were set forth in the Bill of Rights, which was added to the Constitution by amendment a few years later.

SECRETARY OF STATE

George Washington was elected the first President of the United States in 1788; he took office early the following year. By the time Jefferson returned to the United States from Paris in November of 1789, Washington had a new job for him. He asked Jefferson to become the country's first secretary of state.

Jefferson accepted. Before he took up his new duties, however, he had family business to attend to. His daughter, Patsy, having long since given up her plan of becoming a nun, was getting married.

Jefferson's Daughters

Patsy, or Martha as she was called now that she was older, was a talented, intelligent young woman. Tall and red-haired, she resembled her father. She married Thomas Mann Randolph, a second cousin and a member of the Randolph family to which Jefferson's mother had belonged. He was a well-to-do planter who later served as governor of Virginia.

The other of Jefferson's two surviving children, Polly (Mary), was quieter and more delicate; she is said to have resembled her mother. In 1797, she married John Wayles

Eppes, who later became a member of the United States House of Representatives.

Both girls received educations that were considered quite good for the 18th century, when women were not expected to have careers or contribute to public life. Although Jefferson was a liberal, modern thinker in many ways, it would be a mistake to believe that he was completely modern. On some subjects, he shared the opinions held by most people of his generation. One such subject was the role of women. He felt that the proper place for women was in the home, where their purpose was "to soothe and calm the minds of their husbands." His daughters, like most women of the period, accepted this view and turned their energies to managing their households and raising their children.

The President's Cabinet

After Martha's wedding, Jefferson reported for duty as secretary of state at Federal Hall, in the country's temporary capital of New York City. Not long after, the capital was moved to Philadelphia, which pleased Jefferson because he preferred the cultured atmosphere of the Pennsylvania city to the bustling commercialism of New York. But some developments during the next few years were less to his liking.

At the time, the President's Cabinet, like the presidency itself, was a brand-new institution. It consisted of four members. Jefferson was secretary of state. The secretary of war was Henry Knox, a friend of Washington and the founder of the West Point Military Academy. The attorney general was Edmund Randolph. And the secretary of the treasury was New Yorker Alexander Hamilton. Within a short time, Hamilton and Jefferson were to become enemies.

First, though, Jefferson had to determine just what his duties as secretary of state were supposed to be. The primary

The nation's first Cabinet was appointed by President George Washington (far right). It consisted of (from left to right) Henry Knox (seated), Jefferson, Edmund Randolph, and Alexander Hamilton. (Library of Congress.)

responsibility of the secretary of state was—and still is—diplomacy, or relations with foreign powers. During the first years of the Cabinet, however, the secretary of state was also responsible for domestic matters—that is, for all affairs within the United States that did not fall into the domains of the secretaries of war and the treasury. Jefferson had an annual budget of $10,000 and a handful of employees. He set to work immediately on the many concerns that demanded his attention.

In the area of foreign relations, Jefferson's biggest job was dealing with France and Great Britain. These two countries were involved in a long, intermittent war, and each wanted the United States on its side. Jefferson urged President Washington to preserve close, friendly relations with France and to be wary of England.

All his life, Jefferson was to remain partial to France, partly because he felt a kinship of revolutionary ideas between the two countries and partly because he simply loved much about the French people and culture. The violently anti-British feelings he had expressed in the Declaration of Independence stayed with him also, and he did not want the United States to become too friendly with its former oppressor.

In domestic matters, Jefferson soon began to disagree with many of Hamilton's economic ideas and policies. In particular, he disliked Hamilton's plan to raise money through new taxes to pay America's debts to nations that had helped with loans during the Revolutionary War. He believed that Hamilton was pressing too hard the federal government's right to tax the people, and he feared that the new national taxes would be as great and unfair a burden to farmers and settlers as British taxes had been.

Hamilton, in turn, criticized Jefferson's recommendations on foreign policy. He disapproved of the violence of the French Revolution and urged Washington not to become too friendly with France. Alliances with Great Britain, Hamilton felt, would be wiser and more profitable. During the first years of the new constitutional government, the differences of opinion between Jefferson and Hamilton gave rise to a new and unexpected feature of American political life: political parties.

Republicans and Federalists

The authors of the Constitution had not foreseen the rise of political parties, and many Americans were uneasy about the very idea of distinct political parties. They feared that splitting the nation's leadership into separate groups would lead to conflict, strife, and disunity. These feelings were especially strong in the wake of the many conflicts between Whigs and Tories (patriots and those loyal to England) during the American Revolution.

Jefferson was among those who scorned the notion of parties. "If I could not get to heaven but with a party," he once told a friend, "I would not go there at all." Yet he found that, in the free and open exchange of ideas that accompanied the birth of the United States, conflicting opinions emerged and attracted followers. Early in the 1790s, people began to group around his ideas and those of Hamilton. This was the birth of the party system in American politics.

The underlying difference in the thinking of Jefferson and Hamilton involved the powers of the federal government. Jefferson, along with his friend Madison, believed that if the federal government became too strong the rights of the states and of individuals could be threatened. They maintained that the federal government possessed only those powers specifically granted to it by the Constitution.

The people who shared Jefferson's and Madison's view began to be called Democratic-Republicans, or simply Republicans. They stood for states' rights, a cautious and narrow interpretation of the Constitution, and, generally, for good relations with France. The Republicans favored France because of its new revolutionary government and its long-standing opposition to England. Jefferson was acknowledged as the leading thinker and political representative of the Republicans.

Opposed to the Republicans were the Federalists, led by Hamilton. The Federalists argued that the federal government possessed broad powers—that is, that it could take whatever measures were not specifically prohibited by the Constitution. The Federalists favored a strong central government and, generally, good relations with Great Britain. They felt that, in spite of the American Revolution, the United States still had more in common with England than with any other country. Moreover, the stable, prosperous British government offered a good example to the new nation. John Adams, who was Vice-President under Washington, was also a leading Federalist.

Media Mudslinging

The growing split between the two parties found a public voice in the newspapers of the time. One of Jefferson's employees in the State Department was a French translator and poet named Philip Freneau, who was also a newspaper publisher. His paper, the *National Gazette,* attacked Hamilton and the Federalists mercilessly, accusing them of snobbery, aristocratic tendencies, and the secret desire to take the power of self-government away from the American people.

The Federalists, in turn, attacked the Republicans in the pages of the *Gazette of the United States.* Its articles accused Jefferson and his followers of being immoral madmen whose ideas were dangerous to the government and to public security. The *Gazette of the United States* sometimes referred to President Washington as "His Highness" or "His Excellence," a practice that infuriated Jefferson with its echoes of European-style monarchy.

As time went on, it became clear that President Washington was inclined to favor the Federalist point of view over that of the Republicans. Hamilton claimed that the vicious partisan warfare of the newspapers was damaging the prestige of the new government, and Washington agreed. They urged Jefferson to fire or at least to subdue Freneau, but he refused. This was one reason Jefferson grew disgusted with his Cabinet appointment and began to think of resigning. Another reason presented itself in the spring of 1793.

The Calamity of Genêt

France wanted the United States as an ally in its war with England; England wanted the United States to be *its* ally. Unwilling to become caught up in the destructive affairs of the two European nations, Washington declared that the United States would remain neutral. Even Jefferson, who had hoped the United States would side with France against England, accepted the wisdom of this move.

Then France's new ambassador arrived in the United States. His name was Edmond Genêt, and he proved to be a rather poor diplomat. He secretly paid to equip American ships as privateers, or privately owned warships, against England. He also criticized Washington's policy of neutrality, calling the President an enemy of liberty. Genêt stirred up Republican support for France throughout the country and even incited mass rallies and demonstrations in the streets. All of this, of course, was good ammunition for the Federalists, who gloated, "See, it is just as we have said! These French-loving Republicans are hot-tempered, lacking in judgment, given over to mob rule, and maybe even treasonous."

The Genêt incident angered and embarrassed Jefferson. His sympathies truly lay with the French, but he felt that this particular Frenchman was a bumbling oaf. "Never in my opinion," he wrote, "was so calamitous an appointment made as that of the present minister of France here." Weary of the battles and fiascos of public life, Jefferson resigned from the Cabinet in 1793, at the end of President Washington's first term. He parted from the President and returned to Virginia. Once again, he entered a period of retirement at his home on the "little mountain."

VICE-PRESIDENT JEFFERSON

At first, Jefferson's retirement was untroubled by party or political squabbles. He strolled and rode around his plantation and continued the unending series of changes and additions to Monticello. He enjoyed the visits of his older daughter and her children, and he watched his younger daughter fall in love and prepare for her own marriage. He boasted to friends that he no longer even read the *National Gazette* or the *Gazette of the United States*. As for a return to political life, it was out of the question. "I cherish tranquility too much to suffer political things to enter my mind at all," he claimed.

This claim was not quite true. Jefferson certainly engaged in vigorous correspondence with friends throughout the United States, even with President Washington. He discussed political as well as philosophical and personal topics in his letters, and, as time went by, he began to take a renewed interest in the national news.

Federalist Blunders

As Jefferson saw it, the Federalists were making some big mistakes. He had disapproved of one of Hamilton's pet projects, a tax on whiskey, because he felt that it placed too great a hardship on the farmers who grew the grain that was used to make the whiskey. Now it appeared that the farmers shared Jefferson's disapproval. In July of 1794, a group of farmers in western Pennsylvania armed themselves and rebelled against paying the whiskey tax. Washington and Hamilton called for 15,000 militiamen to crush the uprising, which ended peacefully when the farmers laid down their arms and went home.

The Whiskey Rebellion, as the uprising was called, outraged Jefferson. He felt it was ridiculous for the government to react so strongly against its own citizens. The real evil, he claimed, was not in the uprising but in the unjust tax that had prompted it.

The Federalists annoyed Jefferson a second time in 1794 by signing a treaty with Great Britain. Called Jay's Treaty because it was negotiated by John Jay, it gave the United States control of some British forts in the Northwest Territories. However, Jefferson objected to the treaty because it also agreed to trade terms that were very favorable to Great Britain and less favorable to the United States. On top of the Whiskey Rebellion, Jay's Treaty convinced Jefferson that the Federalists were making a mess of things. He began to wonder what would happen in 1796, the year of the next presidential election.

The Election of 1796

In 1796, the Constitution had not yet been amended to limit the number of terms a President could serve. Many people expected Washington to serve for a third term, but he declared that he would not run again. He refused partly because he felt that two terms were enough for any President, and partly because he was tired and wanted to retire to his home at Mount Vernon. The field was wide open, and immediately the Republicans urged Jefferson to consider running for President.

At first, Jefferson claimed that he was not interested. He suggested that Madison run. But Madison pointed out that Jefferson was famous as the author of the Declaration of Independence and widely regarded as the founder of Republican principles. Madison felt that Jefferson would have a better chance of beating the Federalists.

The Federalist candidate was John Adams, who had been Washington's Vice-President for two terms. The relationship between Adams and Jefferson in 1796 was a troubled one. The two had become friends in the glorious days of 1776, when Jefferson had written the Declaration of Independence and Adams had defended it on the floor of the Continental Congress. Even after they became members of opposing political parties, they remained cordial to one another for a while.

Then, in the early 1790s, Jefferson wrote the introduction to a new edition of Thomas Paine's book *The Rights of Man*. Jefferson hinted in his introduction that the book was a good response to some recent Federalist essays that had been written by Adams. After the book was published, a series of anonymous letters appeared in the newspapers attacking Jefferson and praising Adams. Jefferson thought that Adams had written the letters, but it was Adams' son, John Quincy Adams, who really was the author. These letters provoked a quarrel between the arch-Republican Jefferson and the arch-Federalist Adams that was to last for many years.

As the election of 1796 approached, Madison and other Republicans, including Aaron Burr of New York, began a newspaper campaign on Jefferson's behalf. Without ever formally agreeing to run for President, Jefferson found himself emerging as the Republican candidate. When the votes of the electoral college (the group of electors, chosen by the citizens of each state, who actually elect the President and Vice-President) were counted, Adams had 71, the highest number cast for any candidate. Jefferson had 68, the second-highest number.

Under the electoral rules of the time, the President and Vice-President were not elected on separate ballots. Instead, the candidate who received the highest number of votes became President; the candidate with the second-highest number became Vice-President — even if they belonged to different parties. The election of 1796 made Federalist John Adams the second President of the United States and Republican Thomas Jefferson his Vice-President. Burr, who had hoped to be Vice-President under Jefferson, went home to New York to practice law.

A New Job and a New Capital

Jefferson went to Philadelphia in February of 1797 to be sworn in as Vice-President. He knew, however, that the nation's capital would not long remain in Philadelphia. During Washington's first term, a site had been chosen, on the Potomac River between Maryland and Virginia, for a new capital city.

The new capital, called Washington, was under construction when Adams took office as President, and he was the first President to live in the new President's House, now called the White House. As an enthusiastic amateur architect and city planner, Jefferson had made some contributions to the new city: locations for buildings, names for streets and other features, and the like. He had also suggested that the height of buildings be limited, as they were in parts of Paris, to ensure air and light in the streets; this suggestion was adopted and is still followed in Washington, D.C., today.

Most of Jefferson's four-year term as Vice-President was not as entertaining as planning the new capital. Like Adams before him and many Vice-Presidents after him, Jefferson found the job to be empty and somewhat boring. His only real duty was to preside over the Senate, and he carried out this task with fairness and punctuality. In fact, because he could never keep from recording and improving whatever he set his hand to, he wrote a handbook of guidelines for correct procedures in the meetings of the Senate. It is called *A Manual of Parliamentary Practice,* and it is still used in the Senate.

Conflict with France

The years of Jefferson's vice-presidency were notable chiefly for the threat of war with France, a threat that President Adams had managed to avert. France was disappointed and angry that the United States had resumed cordial relations with England. Because France and England were now at war, France was disposed to regard England's allies as its own enemies. French ships began engaging in skirmishes with American vessels on the high seas.

At the same time, many Americans were horrified by the excesses of the French Revolution, during which thousands of people were beheaded by the guillotine. Americans became even more outraged when Talleyrand, the French foreign minister, insulted U.S. ministers by demanding a huge loan for France and a personal bribe for himself before allowing discussion of a treaty between the two nations. Adams had to steer a careful course to keep the United States out of war.

The Alien and Sedition Acts

The troubled relationship between France and the United States, and the threat of war, led to passage of two congressional acts that disturbed Jefferson deeply. The first was the Alien Act, passed in 1798. It allowed the President to expel from the country any alien (non-U.S. citizen) suspected of being dangerous to the national security. Some of the people deported under the Alien Act were French, many of whom were supporters of the Republican Party.

The second law was the Sedition Act, passed around the same time as the Alien Act. It allowed the President to order fines or imprisonment for anyone convicted of publishing malicious statements about the President or the government. Under the Sedition Act, strongly worded criticism could be viewed as treason.

To Jefferson and other Republicans, the Alien and Sedition Acts were a violation of an individual's right to freedom of opinion and freedom of speech. In passing these laws, Jefferson felt that the Federalist-dominated Congress had proven itself as tyrannical as the British government before the Revolution. He struck back at Congress by writing a protest against the two acts. Although the protest did not bear Jefferson's name and was presented by some of his friends, many people knew that it was the work of the Vice-President. In his protest, Jefferson argued that a state could overturn or ignore a law passed by Congress if that law violated the Constitution. Because the protest was presented to the state legislatures of Kentucky and Virginia, it came to be called the Kentucky and Virginia Resolution.

Many people shared Jefferson's opinion of the Alien and Sedition Acts; even some Federalists felt that Adams had gone too far. The acts were quietly repealed, first in Kentucky and then in other states. They were generally regarded as a mistake and an embarrassment for the Federalists. But they had one important effect—they convinced Jefferson that the Federalists must be removed from power in the 1800 election.

Chapter **6**

The Philosopher as President

The presidential campaign of 1800 was fueled by the hostility the Federalists and Republicans felt for one another. The arguments of each party tended to turn on the personalities and characteristics of the other party's candidate. Federalist newspapers and pamphlets usually portrayed Jefferson as a drunkard, an atheist (someone who does not believe in God), and an unruly anarchist (a person who is opposed to all forms of government). Republican newspapers and pamphlets, on the other hand, portrayed Adams as a cruel tyrant, wearing a crown and waving a scepter (symbols of kingship).

The chief political issue of the campaign was the question of states' rights and the power of the federal government. Adams wanted to uphold a strong central government. Jefferson, the author of the Kentucky and Virginia Resolutions, was clearly a states' rights man.

THE VOTES ARE CAST

In the years before 1800, the Federalist Party had been weakened by fighting between Adams and Hamilton. As a result, the Federalists in the electoral college did not rally behind Adams. Some voted for him, but others voted for Charles Cotesworth Pinckney, another Federalist candidate. And New York State's 12 electoral votes, which had been cast for the Federalist candidate in 1796, went to Jefferson because Republicans now outnumbered Federalists in the New York legislature. When the votes were counted, the Republicans had won a clear victory. John Adams would not serve a second term as President.

The election was not smooth sailing for the Republicans, however. They had to settle a conflict within their own party. Jefferson and Aaron Burr each received 73 electoral votes — but which of the two would be President and which Vice-President? The electoral system then in use did not specify that a given vote was cast for a particular office.

During the campaign, it had been quite clear that the Republicans were proposing Jefferson for President and Burr for Vice-President. But once he saw how many votes he had received, Burr refused to concede the presidency to Jefferson. So the Republicans won the election, only to argue among themselves over who was to be President.

Hamilton the Tie-Breaker

The rules of the electoral college called for a tied electoral vote to be settled by an election in the House of Representatives. Each state was to cast one vote, which was decided by a majority vote of that state's delegates. It took six days in February of 1801 for the House to agree on the next President.

The first 35 ballots failed to produce a winner. Finally, Alexander Hamilton used his considerable powers of persuasion to swing the 36th ballot in Jefferson's favor. As a Federalist, Hamilton intensely disliked both Jefferson and Burr, but he felt that Jefferson was less dangerous. (Hamilton was correct in at least a personal sense; four years later, Burr shot and killed Hamilton in a duel.) Thus, largely through the intervention of a political enemy, Jefferson became the third President of the United States, with Burr as his Vice-President.

Inauguration

Jefferson was inaugurated into the presidency in Washington on March 4, 1801. He walked from his boardinghouse to the Capitol building, where the ceremony took place. His inaugural speech was a plea for tolerance and unity among the various parties and classes of Americans, who, he reminded them, shared a common love of liberty.

> Let us then, fellow citizens, unite with one heart and one mind. Let us restore to social intercourse that harmony and affection without which liberty and even life itself are but dreary things. And let us reflect that, having banished from our land that religious intolerance under which mankind so long bled and suffered, we have yet gained little if we countenance a political intolerance as despotic, as wicked, and capable of as bitter and bloody persecutions. . . . We are all Republicans, we are all Federalists.

First Steps

Jefferson's first task was to move into the large stone President's House on Pennsylvania Avenue as soon as the Adamses had moved out. The President's House, although not as large as it is today, was a graceful and attractive building. But it was one of the few things in Washington at that time that *was* attractive.

The area set aside for the nation's capital proved to be swampy, damp, and fever-ridden. Pennsylvania Avenue was a muddy strip of tree stumps and wagon ruts. And the tops of only a handful of new brick buildings rose above the mire of construction and the rubble of workmen's shacks. The spacious, elegant capital city envisioned by its planners was just beginning to take shape and would not emerge for several years. Nevertheless, because the capital was an exciting, stimulating place to be, Jefferson was able to gather capable men to act as his Cabinet and aides.

Jefferson's first step was to give the important post of secretary of state to his old friend James Madison. Robert Smith, a Maryland lawyer, was named secretary of the Navy, a post that had been created during Adams' presidency. Jefferson gave the post of secretary of the treasury to Swiss-born Albert Gallatin, a financial genius who could solve the problem of the national debt if anyone could. Henry Dearborn of Maine, who had been an officer in the Continental Army, was named secretary of war. Levi Lincoln of Massachusetts was appointed attorney general. By appointing Dearborn and Lincoln to his Cabinet, Jefferson hoped to increase his support in the New England states, which were traditionally strongholds of Federalism. Jefferson also appointed as his private secretary a young Virginian, an Army captain named Meriwether Lewis.

CHALLENGES AT HOME AND ABROAD

Critics of Jefferson claimed that he was a dreamy, starry-eyed philosopher with no gift for practical government. They pointed to his troubles as governor of Virginia as evidence that he lacked the ability to make decisions and get things done. Jefferson, however, was soon to prove them wrong. His administration was notable for daring decisions and extraordinary activity.

The Revolution of 1800

Jefferson's election to the presidency has been called the Revolution of 1800, because the fall of Federalism and the rise of Republicanism ushered in a number of changes in the country's government and general atmosphere. Jefferson set out to undo some of the harm the Federalists had caused.

He repealed the federal tax on liquor that had sparked the Whiskey Rebellion. He made sure that the Alien and Sedition Acts lapsed and were not renewed. He made it easier for foreigners to become American citizens by reducing to five years the time they were required to live in the United States before becoming eligible for citizenship. And he prevented a number of Federalist judges who had been appointed by Adams from taking office.

Jefferson also banished the formality and splendor of official occasions that had been encouraged by the Federalists, particularly by Washington, because he felt that this pomp and ceremony smacked of aristocratic privilege. In its place, he introduced the plainness and informality that he believed more appropriate to a republic. It is possible that on some occasions Jefferson went a bit too far in the direction of informality. When Anthony Merry, the British minister to the United States, called on the President, he was shocked to find him wearing shabby house slippers and grubby, disheveled clothes.

War Against the Barbary Pirates

No sooner had Jefferson taken office than he faced a challenge from far-off Africa. At that time, the Mediterranean coast of North Africa, in the region that is now the countries of Libya, Tunisia, Morocco, and Algeria, was called the Barbary Coast. This name came not from the word "barbarian," as is sometimes mistakenly supposed, but from the name of the native peoples, who were called Berbers. The Barbary Coast was ruled by Turkey, but—for a price—the Turkish over-lords were willing to share their power with certain local pirate chiefs.

These pirates haunted the Barbary Coast from their hideout in Tripoli, the capital of present-day Libya. They preyed upon shipping in the busy Mediterranean sea-lanes through a kind of maritime extortion, demanding high fees from all nations in exchange for the safe passage of their ships. Like most countries, the United States had decided it was easier to pay this "tribute" than to risk piracy and war. Jefferson disapproved of paying the pirates, but he continued the practice during his first few months in office. Then, in May of 1801, the Tripolitanians raised the price of safe passage and demanded greater fees.

Jefferson was furious. Because he believed the so-called Tripolitanian "sultans" were nothing more than rascally pirates, he refused to pay another cent of "tribute". Tripoli then declared war on the United States, whereupon Jefferson sent naval vessels and men of the U.S. Marine Corps (founded by Adams in 1798) to Tripoli to protect American ships and attack the pirates.

For some time, nothing much happened on either side in the Tripolitanian War. But the United States suffered a set-back in 1803 when the pirates seized the American gunship *Philadelphia*, threw its crew into prison, and attacked the rest of the U.S. fleet.

In 1804, Lieutenant Stephen Decatur of the U.S. Navy turned the tide of the Tripolitanian War in a daring raid. He sailed along the Barbary Coast, firing on pirate ships as he went, and set fire to the *Philadelphia*. After losing their prize of war, the Tripolitanians also lost heart. The following year

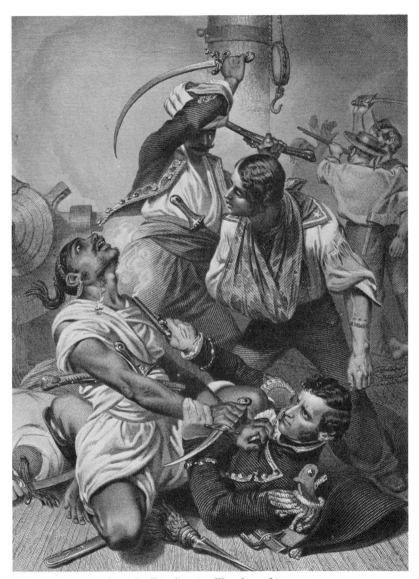

This exciting scene from the Tripolitanian War shows Lieutenant Stephen Decatur of the U.S. Navy firing a pistol at the pirate who pins him to the deck of the Philadelphia, *while an heroic young seaman thrusts himself in front of another pirate's cutlass to save his commander.* (Library of Congress.)

they agreed to give up their demands for "tribute"—although Jefferson still had to pay $60,000 to ransom the crew of the *Philadelphia*.

The Tripolitanian War was considered the United States' first victory on foreign soil. Part of the first line of the Marine Corps hymn, which begins, "From the halls of Montezuma, to the shores of Tripoli," refers to this victory. It was a costly victory, though, and Jefferson decided it would be easier to go on paying the "tribute" fees demanded by Algeria, Morocco, and Tunisia. By about 1815, however, the large-scale sea battles of Europe's Napoleonic Wars had pretty much wiped out the pirates of the Barbary Coast.

THE LOUISIANA PURCHASE

Without a doubt, the most important and exciting event of Jefferson's administration was the Louisiana Purchase, a surprising and shrewd triumph of timing and policy that more than doubled the size of the United States with the stroke of a pen. The key players in this diplomatic drama were Jefferson; Napoleon Bonaparte, the First Consul of France; and two Americans in Paris, Robert R. Livingston and Jefferson's old friend and former assistant, James Monroe.

Jefferson had long been curious about the French-owned land west of the Mississippi River and wondered what part, if any, it would play in the development of the United States. His enthusiasm for all things French had cooled a bit with the rise to power of the empire-building Napoleon, and he feared the First Consul's ambitions.

Having conquered most of Europe, Napoleon, many people thought, might next turn his attention to the French territories in America—and, perhaps, even to the United States. Jefferson hoped to head off any such turn of events. He instructed Livingston, the U.S. minister in France, to offer Napoleon $10 million in exchange for part of West Florida and the port of New Orleans at the mouth of the Mississippi.

Napoleon's Surprising Response

To Jefferson's amazement, Napoleon made a counteroffer. He indicated that he might be willing to sell not just New Orleans but the entire Louisiana Territory! This was a tremendous tract of land—no one knew exactly how large—between the Mississippi River and the Rocky Mountains (then called the Stony Mountains).

Napoleon had several reasons for wanting to sell the center of North America to the United States. He was once again on the brink of war with England and needed money to pay for troops and other expenses. With his hands full in Europe, Napoleon probably felt that he could not afford to overextend himself. Perhaps he was further discouraged from adventures in the New World by his failure in 1802 to hold onto the French colony of Sainte-Domingue (present-day Haiti) on the Caribbean island of Hispaniola after the colony had risen up against the French in a bloody slave revolt.

Because Livingston had not yet been able to come to definite terms with Napoleon, Jefferson sent Monroe to France to help with the negotiations. Monroe had served as an ambassador to France in the 1790s and was well liked by the French. Jefferson hoped that Monroe's presence in France would speed up the negotiations.

As it turned out, Napoleon and Livingston agreed on a purchase price for the Louisiana Territory just before Monroe arrived in France in early 1803. But Monroe and Livingston together worked out the detailed treaty provisions of what has come to be called the Louisiana Purchase. For a total of $15 million, the United States bought 828,000 square miles of unexplored territory, much of it rich farmland. The Louisiana Purchase gave the United States title to all of present-day Louisiana, Missouri, Arkansas, Iowa, South Dakota, North Dakota, Nebraska, and Oklahoma, as well as most of Kansas, Wyoming, Colorado, Montana, and Minnesota. While signing the treaty of sale on behalf of the United States, Livingston remarked to Monroe, "We have lived long, but this is the noblest work of our whole lives."

Napoleon, too, was pleased. He had $15 million to spend, and he was happy to think that the United States, in growing larger and stronger, would give England a formidable adversary in the New World. "I have just given England a maritime power that sooner or later will lay low her pride," Napoleon is reported to have said as he congratulated himself on the signing of the treaty.

The Question of Constitutionality

The Louisiana Purchase, however, did pose one vexing problem for Jefferson. As a Republican who had always favored a very narrow and cautious interpretation of the Constitution, he had difficulty justifying the purchase on constitutional grounds. Nowhere in the Constitution was the President given the power to obtain territories by treaty. But he had instructed Monroe and Livingston to act quickly, without waiting to refer the matter to Congress for its approval, in order to take advantage of Napoleon's fickle moods.

When the treaty arrived from France, Jefferson decided to sign it first and let Congress argue over it later. He claimed that he acted out of the urgent need to secure a safe border and to provide for future growth. However, a few of his harshest critics complained that the Louisiana Purchase was only a plot to add more Republican states to the Union. But they were shouted down by the outburst of public approval that greeted the announcement of the purchase. Nearly all Americans agreed that the Louisiana Purchase was a remarkable real estate deal and an unbeatable bargain. Fortunately, the Senate later ratified the purchase (accepted it as law) by a large majority.

EXPLORING THE WILD WEST

The vast, unexplored western reaches of the continent beckoned and enticed Americans as the eastern seaboard grew more populous and the frontier inched toward the Mississippi River. (Ohio, the only state to enter the Union during Jefferson's presidency, achieved statehood in 1803 under the terms of the plan he had drawn up years before in the Continental Congress.)

With the explorer's imagination that he had inherited from his mapmaker father, Jefferson shared the public's fascination with the western frontier. Even before the Louisiana Purchase, he had begun making plans for an expedition into the unknown West. He had made Meriwether Lewis his personal secretary with the thought that Lewis would be a good choice to lead such an expedition. He had even sent Lewis to Philadelphia to study botany, zoology, and navigation by the stars. Now, with the ink barely dry on the Louisiana Purchase, there was no reason to wait any longer. Jefferson asked Lewis to lead the first overland expedition to the far West Coast of the continent.

Lewis and Clark

Lewis agreed, but suggested that a share of the expedition's command be given to William Clark, another Virginian and an army officer. Jefferson approved, and the journey that resulted, one of the most famous in history, was known as the Lewis and Clark Expedition. Lewis was 29 when they set out; Clark was 33.

Late in 1803, the leaders assembled the expedition in St. Louis, which was at that time at the edge of the frontier. They had a crew of about 40 men, including Clark's black slave, many tons of supplies, including medicine, ammunition, and presents for Indians, and three large river boats. Their plan was to travel northwest by water up the Missouri River to its source, and then into the uncharted regions beyond.

Jefferson has given Lewis and Clark very detailed instructions. They were to observe and record the appearance and customs of the Indians; they were to map the geography of the West and keep careful notes of their route; they were to study and bring back samples of the plants, animals, and minerals they found along the way; and, for good measure, they might as well report on the climate, weather, economic potential, and natural or human wonders of the lands they passed through. In addition, they were to determine once and for all whether or not there was such a thing as a Northwest Passage—the fabled, easy water route across the continent to the Pacific Ocean that explorers had dreamed of since Columbus' day.

Lewis and Clark spent the winter making their preparations in St. Louis. Then, on May 14, 1804, their journal records, they "Set out at 4 o'clock P.M., in the presence of many of the neighbouring inhabitents, and proceeded on under a jentle brease up the Missourie." Soon they had passed out of all knowledge of their countrymen. When months passed and no word of them reached the waiting nation, they were given up for dead. In Washington, Jefferson grieved for the loss of these brave men. The year 1804 brought him other causes for grief as well.

TWO TRAGEDIES

Jefferson's younger daughter, Mary, died in 1804 after giving birth to her second child. Jefferson mourned her deeply. In spite of the coldness that had developed between him and John Adams, he received a letter of condolence on his loss from Adams' wife, Abigail, who had looked after Mary years before when she arrived in Europe to join her father.

The second tragedy of 1804 concerned Jefferson's Vice-President, Aaron Burr, and his old enemy, Alexander Hamilton. Relations between Jefferson and Burr had been strained ever since Burr had refused to concede the presidency to Jefferson in 1800. As the election of 1804 approached, Jefferson asked George Clinton of New York to run for Vice-President; he did not intend, if he were re-elected, to spend the next four years with a Vice-President he disliked and distrusted. Knowing that he was soon to be out of a job, Burr ran for governor of New York but was defeated, largely because of Hamilton's opposition. The campaign grew rather heated, and personal insults were exchanged. Then Burr challenged Hamilton to a duel.

Hamilton, who disapproved of dueling, accepted the challenge so as not to seem a coward. But on July 11, when the duel was fought in New Jersey, Hamilton fired his pistol into the air, believing that Burr could not possibly be serious. Burr was quite serious, however; he shot to kill and fatally wounded Hamilton, who died the next day. Burr, his reputation destroyed and his career ended, fled to the West.

Rumors of Treason

This violent episode shocked the American public and the government; it also dismayed Jefferson. As much as he had detested Hamilton, Jefferson certainly had no wish to see him meet such a sad and violent end. But worse was to follow.

Burr, in his exile, spent several years trying to enlist support for a wild plan—a plan that he falsely claimed was secretly sponsored by President Jefferson. Burr wanted to invade the Louisiana Purchase territory and provoke war with Spain over the region that is now Texas. The details of his plot have never been fully uncovered, but it is more than likely that Burr intended to set up an independent republic somewhere in the West, with himself as its head of state. Jefferson was alarmed and extremely angry. He felt that his former Vice-President was not only a murderer but also a traitor, and certainly a disgrace to the high office he had once held.

Burr was arrested for treason in 1807 and stood trial before Chief Justice John Marshall. Although Jefferson hoped for a conviction, Burr was found not guilty and set free. He spent several years in Europe, then returned to New York and his law practice in 1812.

As Jefferson's first term drew to a close and the election of 1804 approached, the President could look back on a lively four years. He had put some of his Republican principles into action at home. He had the Tripoli pirates on the run at last. He had made the largest land purchase in history for about three cents an acre. He had lost an enemy and a Vice-President in dramatic circumstances. And he had launched one of the most daring journeys of exploration of all time, even though its fate was still a mystery.

Chapter 7

The President's House Again

Jefferson had told friends after the 1800 election that he intended to serve only one term as President. But he decided in 1804 that he would serve a second term if elected. Perhaps this decision was based on the expectation that he would be elected quite easily. He was popular with the people and had enjoyed some successes during his first term—particularly the Louisiana Purchase. At any rate, Jefferson was nominated unanimously as the Republican candidate in February of 1804.

The election of 1804 was different from previous presidential elections in one important way. After the confusing election of 1800, when Jefferson and Burr had tied in the electoral balloting and then fought over the presidency, everyone agreed that the system needed to be changed to prevent such a thing from happening again. As a result, the 12th Amendment to the Constitution was passed in 1804. Under this amendment, the electors voted separately for the President and the Vice-President, so there could be no doubt about who held which office.

THE ELECTION OF 1804

As soon as he decided to run again, Jefferson picked George Clinton as the vice-presidential candidate to replace the unsatisfactory Burr. Clinton was a New York lawyer who had served in the Continental Congress, commanded a militia regiment against the British, and been governor of New York from 1777 to 1795 and again from 1801 to 1804.

The Federalists mounted a feeble challenge. Their presidential candidate, Charles Cotesworth Pinckney of South Carolina, was an intelligent and qualified man. He had been captured by the British during the Revolution and later had served at the Constitutional Convention and as a minister to France. But Federalism had lost much of its popular support, especially after an incident that came to be known as the Essex Junto. In this ill-planned and ill-fated venture, a group of extreme Federalists in Massachusetts tried to secede from the Union, urging neighboring regions to leave the United States and form a New England Confederacy. The Essex Junto failed in its secession attempt; it succeeded only in drawing the scorn of the American public to the Federalist Party.

The election of 1804, with Jefferson very popular and the Federalists discredited, was one of the most uneven in American history. Jefferson received 162 electoral votes; Pinckney, 14. Jefferson won the majority of electoral votes in 15 of the 17 states. The President's House would continue to be a Republican's residence.

Jefferson was inaugurated for his second term in Washington on March 4, 1805. His inaugural address this time dealt largely with the Louisiana Purchase of several years earlier. Still touchy about accusations that he had acted in an unconstitutional way, he defended the purchase, saying, "But who can limit the extent to which the federative principle may operate effectively? The larger our association the less will it be shaken by local passions; and in any view is it not better that the opposite bank of the Mississippi should be settled by our own brethren and children than by strangers of another family?"

JEFFERSON'S SECOND TERM

At the beginning of his second term, Jefferson had to find a replacement for Attorney General Levi Lincoln, who wanted to return to Massachusetts politics. John Breckinridge of Kentucky took over the post; he was replaced, in turn, by Caesar Rodney of Delaware in 1807.

Jefferson spent much time in 1805 and 1806 following the activities of Burr on the frontier and trying to have his former Vice-President caught and arrested. When Burr was finally captured in 1807, Attorney General Rodney played a great part in bringing him to trial for treason.

In the course of the Burr trial, Jefferson established an important presidential precedent. The court requested the President to appear at the trial and to present certain documents and papers that might concern the case. Jefferson declined to appear, and he sent only some of the requested papers, claiming that the others affected national security and he would not make them public. The court, unable to force Jefferson to submit all the desired materials, accepted his decision and labeled it "executive privilege." Many Presidents have used the concept of executive privilege since Jefferson's time.

Trouble on the High Seas

The years of 1805 and 1806 also saw an increase in tension abroad and on the high seas. France and England were fighting what were known as the Napoleonic Wars, and Jefferson found it difficult to maintain the neutrality of the United States. Both sides had given up on the idea of obtaining the United States as an ally; now they had a different purpose. Neither side wanted the United States to help the other, either with loans or through trade, so ships of both nations caused problems at sea for American ships. But the relationship between France and the United States remained fairly friendly. This time, England was the worse offender.

The British Navy's policy of impressment was at the core of the problem. After years of war, the British Navy desperately needed sailors, and it adopted desperate methods to obtain them. One such method was impressment, or carrying men onto naval vessels by force. Once aboard, the hapless victims had no choice but to sign up as sailors. Bands of naval agents, called press gangs, roamed the waterfronts and seaside villages of England, looking for idle or unwary prey.

Impressment became an international issue when the dreaded press gangs began impressing American sailors into the British Navy. The British would stop American ships at sea and impress some of the sailors, especially those of British birth who had become naturalized American citizens. The British claimed that these sailors were still British citizens, whether they liked it or not, and were to be treated as deserters. Sometimes the British impressed the entire crews of merchant ships and then sold the vessels and their cargoes.

Americans were outraged at this flagrant abuse of their nation's rights and sovereignty. Some called for war on England. But Jefferson feared that such a war would end badly for the United States. Through James Monroe, who was the American ambassador to England until 1807, Jefferson tried tirelessly to negotiate a solution to the growing problem, but the British remained firm: impressment was their right and there was nothing anyone could do about it. Before long, the problem would become a crisis. First, however, Jefferson was able to enjoy one of the great triumphs of his second administration.

HOW THE WEST WAS WON

On September 23, 1806, after nearly 2½ years, the Lewis and Clark Expedition returned to St. Louis. The explorers had long since been given up for dead, and the townspeople greeted them with wild jubilation. That same day, Lewis sat down and wrote to President Jefferson, telling him that the expedition had returned. Jefferson received the news with what he called "unspeakable joy" and wanted to hear all the men's adventures. The whole nation, indeed, was burning with curiosity. And Lewis and Clark had quite a tale to tell.

Going Out

After leaving St. Louis in May of 1804, the expedition went up the Missouri River to the home of the Mandan Sioux Indians in what is now North Dakota. In November, they built Fort Mandan near a village of friendly Indians and spent the winter there. In the spring of 1805, they made their way, in smaller boats and on foot, to the headwaters of the Missouri in southwestern Montana.

Here, in the territory of the Shoshone Indians, they obtained horses and an Indian guide. Anxious to get through the Rocky Mountains while summer lasted, they pushed westward and crossed the Continental Divide near what is now the U.S.-Canada border. Descending the far side of the stupendous mountain chain, they found a stream they named the Clearwater. They made canoes and followed the Clearwater to a large river, the Snake, which flowed into a still larger river, the Columbia. The Columbia then carried them all the way to the Pacific Ocean, which they reached on November 15, 1805.

Coming Back

The expedition wintered in another newly built fort near what is now Astoria, Oregon, and set off eastward for the trip home in March of 1806. After crossing the Rockies, the expedition split into two groups. One group, led by Lewis, took a northerly route along the Marias River. The other group, led by Clark, took a southerly route along the Yellowstone River. Lewis and Clark later met where the Yellowstone flows into the Missouri, and they journeyed downstream together for the last leg of the trip, the return to St. Louis.

It was an extraordinary trip, one that had not been made before by the English, the French, the Spanish, or—so far as is known—even by the Indians. The accounts of the travelers show that they faced not only difficult terrain and punishing weather but also hostile Indians, grizzly bears, rattlesnakes, mountain lions, starvation and thirst, and sickness. Despite these dangers, only one man was lost, and he died of a ruptured appendix.

The Rewards

All told, the Lewis and Clark Expedition covered about 8,000 miles of unknown territory. True to Jefferson's instructions, its leaders had kept detailed journals, and Clark had made very good maps. Lewis and Clark brought back a treasure house of new information about the exciting, mysterious West. They did much to open the territory up to exploration and settlement. They also laid to rest the myth of the long-sought-after Northwest Passage.

The Story of Sacajawea

Lewis and Clark became national heroes after their return to St. Louis in 1806. A heroine also emerged from the Lewis and Clark Expedition—a brave and resourceful Indian woman named Sacajawea.

When they left Fort Mandan, Lewis and Clark took along a French-Canadian trapper named Toussaint Charbonneau to interpret Indian languages for them. He was allowed to bring his wife, a Shoshone Indian woman called Sacajawea (''Bird Woman''), and their baby son. Although many of the men grumbled at the idea of taking a woman and a baby along on such a dangerous expedition, Sacajawea proved to be far more helpful than her husband at interpreting the languages of the Shoshone and Walla Walla Indians they met along the way. She was especially helpful in winning the friendship of the Shoshone, as she was a member of their tribe.

Sacajawea has sometimes been called the expedition's guide, but that is not strictly accurate. She chose the route only on one occasion, when she accompanied Clark's group to the Yellowstone River area of southwestern Montana and advised Clark to choose a particular mountain pass. But she carried her weight in other ways: by rescuing some valuable supplies from a canoe that overturned in mid-river; by teaching the men how to use roots for food when they were starving; and by demonstrating powers of endurance, intelligence, and courage equal to those of the expedition's leaders. Sacajawea deserves to be remembered as one of America's early heroines.

Lewis and Clark each received 1,600 acres of public land as payment for his services; each later also served a stint as governor of the Louisiana Territory. In 1814, they published their journals as a book called *History of the Expedition Under the Commands of Captains Lewis and Clark*. It became one of America's first best-sellers. It and other documents from the expedition are still valuable for the wealth of information they contain—and still immensely enjoyable for the vivid picture they paint of America's West before the coming of the white man.

EVENTFUL 1807

Two noteworthy events of Jefferson's second administration occurred in 1807. One was a purely domestic matter; it concerned a perplexing moral and ethical problem. The other was an international incident with serious economic and political consequences.

Jefferson and Slavery

The first of these two events concerned the question of slavery. Almost since the founding of the colonies, those in the South had relied on the labor of black African slaves. These colonies had been settled in large part by wealthy British landowners, some of them aristocrats, who were accustomed to having large estates and many servants. Most of the people in the South believed that slavery was not only natural and acceptable but also necessary to make the huge tobacco and cotton plantations productive.

The North, however, had originally been settled by members of the British working and middle classes. It was characterized by small businesses and family farms rather than by large plantations, so slavery was not a part of northern culture. And many northerners believed slavery to be morally wrong. As early as Jefferson's time, an antislavery movement was beginning among churchmen in the North.

Jefferson was a slaveowner. His family had owned slaves all his life, and, at the time of his death, he had about 250 slaves at Monticello. Although he did set some of his slaves free, Jefferson also offered rewards for runaway slaves and punished disobedient ones with whippings, just like any other slaveowner. Because of this, it has sometimes been said that Jefferson's beliefs in liberty and equality—the beliefs he expressed in the Declaration of Independence—were insincere or inconsistent.

The problem of slavery was a difficult one for Jefferson, and here again it would be a mistake to expect a man born and raised in the 18th century to share modern attitudes. In *Notes on the State of Virginia* and in many of his letters, Jefferson made it quite clear that he was thoroughly opposed to slavery, but that he could think of no satisfactory way to end it. In other words, he was against slavery in theory but could not put his beliefs into practice. For Jefferson also felt that black and white people were fundamentally different; he did not believe that they could ever live harmoniously together as equals in the same society.

As Jefferson grew older, the slavery issue continued to plague him. Although he hated slavery, he could not accept the idea of freeing the slaves as a solution to the problem.

He wished it were possible to return American blacks to Africa. Indeed, he later supported the American Colonization Society (ACS), a group founded in 1817 to find new homes in West Africa for freed black slaves. The present-day nation of Liberia started as a colony created by the ACS.

Yet Jefferson knew that any serious attempt to remove all blacks from the United States would not only be extremely difficult but would be blocked by the slaveowners of the South. In March of 1807, he did what he could to curb the growth of slavery by sponsoring a bill that abolished the slave trade. Under this new law, no slaves could be imported into the United States after January 1, 1808; the slave population was limited to the blacks already in America and their descendants. Although slaves continued to be smuggled into the country for the next 60 years, the slave trade was officially ended and the growth of the slave population slowed abruptly.

Jefferson was never able to resolve the conflict in his feelings about slavery. And he feared that it was a conflict that would someday be shared by the nation as a whole. He was one of the first Americans to foresee the coming strife between the free states of the North and the slave states of the South. In 1820, when Congress was battling over the issue of slavery in the newly created western states, Jefferson wrote that his fears about slavery were like "a fire-bell in the night," filling him with dread and alarm for the future of the country. The conflict he foresaw, of course, developed into the Civil War that wracked the nation half a century later.

The *Leopard* and the *Chesapeake*

The second important event of 1807 involved trouble on the high seas. In June, the British frigate *Leopard* ordered the *Chesapeake*, an American naval ship, to halt and be searched for deserters. At the time, the two ships were about 10 miles off the coast of Norfolk, Virginia. After searching the *Chesapeake*, the British commander claimed that four of the American seamen were British deserters. When the Americans refused to turn over the men, the *Leopard* opened fire. Four Americans were killed and many were injured.

The outcry in the United States after this episode was loud and angry. "Never since the battle of Lexington have I seen this country in such a state of exasperation," wrote Jefferson. Many people wanted to declare war on England, but Jefferson refrained. The American Navy was weak, the Army was small, and the country's chances of faring well in such a war did not look good. The President wanted to remain neutral, but he knew that he had to take some action. He chose an economic weapon.

The Embargo Act of 1807

Jefferson decided that the United States could strike a blow at the interfering European powers without going to war by boycotting, or refusing to buy, British or French goods. He thereupon had Congress pass the Embargo Act of 1807. This act prohibited Americans from engaging in any form of trade with either of the two nations, which were the chief trading partners of the United States at that time. This, he felt, would hit England and France where it would hurt the most—in the pocketbook. He hoped that the two nations would then agree to respect the rights of the United States as a neutral power at sea.

Unfortunately, the plan backfired. The embargo on trade had little effect on either England or France, but it did have a devastating effect on the American economy. Sailors, dockworkers, and employees of shipping companies found themselves out of work. Merchants and traders went bankrupt. Farm produce destined for overseas trade rotted in storage sheds. Jefferson's "ograbme" ("embargo" spelled backwards) proved to be the only universally unpopular act of his presidency. Not only did it fail to satisfy those Americans who wanted war to avenge the insult to the *Chesapeake*, but it caused great hardship for many Americans whose livelihoods were threatened. It also failed to accomplish its purpose. Neither France nor England gave any sign that they would welcome a return of trading privileges under terms favorable to U.S. neutrality.

Some critics of the Embargo Act attacked it on philosophical as well as practical grounds. They argued that the right to engage in trade was an important individual freedom. How, then, could Jefferson, the apostle of individual liberty and the foe of a too-strong federal government, overturn that freedom with a federal act? But here Jefferson felt himself to be supported by the Constitution, which gave Congress the power to regulate commerce with other countries in whatever way would best serve national interests.

Such justification did not make the Embargo Act more popular or successful, however. By the time Jefferson's second term entered its final months, he admitted that the embargo had not worked. Shortly before his term of office ended in early 1809, Jefferson approved a new act that lifted most of the restrictions of the Embargo Act. During its 14 months, the embargo had cost the United States an estimated $16 million in customs taxes that would have been paid on foreign goods entering the country, and still more in the money that would have been earned by selling U.S. goods abroad.

THE CAMPAIGN OF 1808

Many historians believe that Jefferson could have been elected easily to a third term. He decided in 1808, however, not to run again. Like Washington, he felt that eight years in the presidency was long enough for any individual. And at age 65, he wanted to return for good to the peace and quiet of Monticello.

Jefferson had long encouraged James Madison, his friend and secretary of state, to prepare himself for the presidency. In 1808, he gave his support to Madison's campaign, and he was happy to see Madison elected in the fall. Jefferson left the President's House in early 1809, confident that Madison, who shared many of his opinions and Republican beliefs, would steer the country on the right course.

In due time, Jefferson was to see the presidency pass to another old Republican friend and fellow Virginian, James Monroe, who succeeded Madison. The Republican "revolution of 1800" that had begun with Jefferson's first election lasted for more than 25 years.

Chapter 8

The Renaissance Man of Monticello

The Renaissance (French for "rebirth") is the name given to the great flowering of learning and the arts in Europe after the long doldrums of the Dark Ages and the Middle Ages. It represents a high-water mark of human energy, ambition, and intelligence. Because of the many areas of life and culture that were illuminated by the Renaissance, we sometimes use the term "Renaissance man" to describe an individual who is gifted and productive in a variety of ways and whose life illustrates the devotion to learning that was the spirit of the Renaissance.

JEFFERSON'S INTERESTS

Thomas Jefferson was such a man, if ever there was one. The range of his interests and accomplishments is staggering. He knew Latin, Greek, French, Italian, Spanish, and Anglo-Saxon (an early forerunner of the English language), and he read and studied works in all these languages. He loved books and assembled several large libraries of rare and modern works. His early love of music lasted throughout his life, as did his violin-playing.

He also enjoyed the study of mathematics, which he claimed to find refreshingly clear and straightforward after the murky confusion of political philosophy. From childhood on, he took an eager interest in natural history. He corresponded with many of the leading scientists of the day, men like the British chemist Joseph Priestley, and he often gave money and time to scientific projects. Once, for example, during his ambassadorship to Paris, he sent an urgent message to friends in the United States requesting them to find, kill, stuff, and ship to him the largest moose they could find so that he could prove a point in a scientific dispute.

Jefferson also continued the study of fossils that he had begun under his early teacher, James Maury. While he was President, he received, examined, and classified a large shipment of fossils from New York State. He also was greatly interested in the early French experiments in ballooning, and he predicted accurately that balloons would someday help man forecast the weather.

The Practical Philosopher

Jefferson's interests were seldom purely theoretical; he was a down-to-earth man and his hobbies usually had a practical side. Although interested in botany and agriculture, for example, he did not confine himself to collecting plant specimens. Instead, he took an active interest in scientific farming and tried a variety of experiments at Monticello. Jefferson never tired of the delights of gardening and agriculture. "Though I am an old man," he once said, "I am but a young gardener."

Jefferson designed a new and more efficient type of plow that won a gold medal from a French agricultural society. With the help of an Italian immigrant neighbor named Philip

Jefferson's proposed design for the seal of the United States proclaims his love of freedom. Some of the elements of the design—the pyramidal eye and the motto E Pluribus Unum—are found today on the seal, which appears on the back side of every one-dollar bill. (Library of Congress.)

Mazzei, he introduced such Italian plants as garlic, orange trees, wine grapes, and endive to the United States, hoping that they would become productive crops in the New World. So eager was Jefferson to find useful new plants that he once smuggled a special variety of rice out of Italy. He also tried to raise Spanish Merino sheep, prized for their luxurious wool, but the animals did not thrive in their new home at Monticello.

Jefferson's practical side is also shown in his love of labor-saving gadgets. He invented many such gadgets, a number of which enjoyed widespread use, but Jefferson did not patent any of them. One was the swivel chair; another was a drawing table with a tilting top, like the tables used by architects and artists today. He also invented a bed that folded up into the wall when not in use, a dumbwaiter (or small elevator) to carry wine and other goods from the cellar up into the house, and a ladder that folded out from the wall for use in winding a clock that was placed high over his front door.

One of Jefferson's favorite inventions was a device he called the polygraph. This was a system of rods that connected two pens. When Jefferson wrote with one of the pens, the second pen would make a perfect copy of whatever he was writing.

The polygraph was very useful to Jefferson in his correspondence and record-keeping. For Jefferson, like many people in colonial America, was a voluminous correspondent. He wrote thousands of letters to his family, friends, and acquaintances. He also kept detailed records of his estate's production, his household and estate finances, the weather, his reading, astronomical observations, and anything else he thought was interesting or important. On top of all this, he managed to find an hour or two for a relaxing, solitary horseback ride almost every day.

THE FINAL RETIREMENT

At several points in his political career, Jefferson had retired from public life to Monticello. Each time, however, he had returned to politics within a few years. But when he came home in 1809, it was to stay. He spent nearly all of the rest of his life pursuing his hobbies and interests on his Virginia hilltop. And Monticello itself must be considered the greatest of all these hobbies.

This gem of a home, set in a three-sided arrangement of outbuildings and gardens, reflects Jefferson's love of order and harmony, as well as his many interests. In designing Monticello, he had used some pictures of buildings in the Palladian, or classical Italian, style. After returning from France in 1789, he added some new touches: higher ceilings, a dome over the central hall, and additional rooms. He then continued to make changes—adding outbuildings and gardens, building underground tunnels to connect the various structures without the need for paths across the lawns, installing his labor-saving devices, rearranging the rooms—almost until the day of his death.

In 1923, Monticello was restored to its original state and opened to the public as a museum. Today it contains hundreds of mementoes of Jefferson's life, and it looks very much as it did in his day. The central hall contains his collections of antlers, rocks and crystals, shells, Indian artifacts brought from far away by Lewis and Clark, fossil bones, and stuffed animal heads. The walls are decorated with paintings and maps. Marble statues, busts, and a model of the Great Pyramid of Egypt stand on pedestals around the room.

The study contains a swivel chair, a tilt-top table, and a polygraph; Jefferson's telescope sits in one window. The bedrooms are brightened by skylights, kept warm by double-paned windows, and kept silent by double doors.

All in all, Monticello was both practical and delightfully comfortable, as well as undeniably elegant. "Mr. Jefferson," wrote a French visitor, "is the first American who has consulted the fine arts to know how he should shelter himself from the weather."

Money Troubles

Jefferson's retirement was not to be a time of undisturbed ease. He left Washington with debts totalling about $24,000. His only income was several thousand dollars each year from the sale of goods produced on his estate: crops, flour, and nails manufactured in a small factory of his design. To raise funds, he sold his personal library to the government for $23,950 after the British had burned the Library of Congress during the War of 1812. The Jefferson Library was carried to Washington in 11 bulging wagons and became the core of a new national library. Sadly, however, much of the Jefferson collection was destroyed in a fire at the Library of Congress in 1851.

Although the sale of his books helped for a while, Jefferson's money troubles continued. At the time of his death, he owed $107,274. His daughter Martha, who inherited Monticello, had to sell the estate to pay the debts.

An Old Friendship Renewed

One of the greatest pleasures of Jefferson's retirement was the renewal of his friendship with John Adams, who had retired to his own home in Quincy, Massachusetts. The two men had been friends during the Revolutionary War, but they had quarrelled in the 1790s and had never patched up their differences. Now, in the 1810s, a mutual friend, Benjamin Rush of Philadelphia, urged them to forget the quarrel and write to one another. They did, and they found that they still had warm regard for each other.

The University of Virginia, in Charlottesville, was Jefferson's last great project and the partial fulfillment of a lifelong vision of public education for all Americans. He raised funds for the school, designed it, and was named its first principal. (Library of Congress.)

For a decade or more, the two aging patriots kept up a lively and extensive correspondence. They discussed the affairs of the day, and they exchanged views on topics ranging from slavery to life after death. They also reminisced about the long-ago days of the American Revolution. Both men realized by the 1820s that they were among the few living reminders of that glorious era when the nation was born. Today, their correspondence is treasured by historians as a valuable window into history.

The University of Virginia

Many years earlier, as a member of the Virginia legislature, Jefferson had proposed a plan for public education throughout the state. Although the plan was not adopted in his lifetime, Jefferson finally was able to see part of it become a reality. In his last great project, he founded the University of Virginia.

Jefferson was able to buy an academy in Charlottesville with money from interested friends and backers. He began planning new buildings and a course of study. In 1816, the state legislature voted to incorporate the school under the name Central College. In 1819, it formally became the University of Virginia. Jefferson was named rector, or principal, of the university. He worked furiously for the next few years attending to every detail of planning and construction.

Jefferson found skilled stoneworkers to carve the ornaments of the buildings. He designed a planetarium for the ceiling of the library. He searched for and found good teachers. And he laid out the curriculum, which did not include religious study.

Jefferson also introduced one new feature that has become almost universal in higher education, the elective course. At the time, schools followed a set curriculum and each student at a given school took the same courses. Jefferson wanted "to leave everyone free to attend whatever branches of instruction he wants, and to decline what he does not want." The University of Virginia opened its doors to its first students in 1825.

Illness and Death

Jefferson was overjoyed at the opening of the university. He regarded it as one of the great achievements of his life – a life which now, he knew, was drawing to a close. He suffered from painful rheumatism and, in early 1826, developed an enlargement, possibly a tumor, of the prostate gland. He had to take laudanum (a liquid medicine containing opium) in order to sleep, and frequent attacks of diarrhea weakened him greatly.

July 4, 1826, was to be a day of special celebration throughout the country. It was the 50th anniversary of the Declaration of Independence. As the Declaration's author, Jefferson was invited to attend a ceremony in Washington, but the 83-year-old former President had to refuse. He was too ill and weak to make the trip. But the invitation prompted him to write his last letter. In it he said, "All eyes are opened, or opening to the rights of man. . . . For ourselves, let the annual return of this day forever refresh our recollection of those rights, and an undiminished devotion to them."

By the time July arrived, Jefferson was confined to his bed. On July 2, he fell into an uneasy sleep, and he slept through most of the next day. He woke in the evening to ask, "Is it the Fourth?" Dr. Robley Dunglison, waiting by his bedside, gently replied, "It soon will be."

Jefferson went back to sleep. He died without waking up sometime during the next day, the half-century anniversary of his Declaration. By a strange and moving coincidence,

John Adams died in Massachusetts on that same day. The two men had been the only signers of the Declaration of Independence to become President.

In accordance with his wishes, Jefferson was buried at Monticello in a simple ceremony. His attention to detail and his love of design had been turned even toward his own death—he had designed his own tombstone and written the inscription he wanted it to bear. It said, "Here was buried Thomas Jefferson, Author of the Declaration of Independence, of the Statute of Virginia for Religious Freedom, and the Father of the University of Virginia." He had insisted that it have "not a word more"; there was no mention of his service as President. Unfortunately, the granite tombstone that Jefferson had designed for himself was almost completely chipped away by souvenir hunters within 50 years of his death. Today, his grave is marked by a larger monument erected by Congress.

PRAISE FROM THE PRESIDENTS

Jefferson was widely admired during his lifetime as a champion of individual liberty, the philosopher of the American Revolution, a man of immense learning, a believer in human worth and dignity, and a wise, careful leader. In the years after his death, he was memorialized in statues, monuments, and tributes of all sorts. But perhaps the praise of later Presidents, showing Jefferson's place in the hearts and minds of all Americans, is the greatest tribute he has received.

"He lives and will live in the memory and gratitude of the wise and good, as a luminary of Science, as a votary of liberty, as a model of patriotism, and as a benefactor of human kind," said James Madison.

Abraham Lincoln said, "All honor to Jefferson—to the

Jefferson on Mount Rushmore

The largest of the many monuments to Thomas Jefferson is Mount Rushmore in southwestern South Dakota—a state that was created from territory purchased by Jefferson in the Louisiana Purchase. Now contained in the 1,278-acre Mount Rushmore National Park, the monument is a high granite cliff face in the rugged Black Hills. Gazing forth from the mountainside are the gigantic 60-foot-tall faces of four American Presidents: George Washington, Thomas Jefferson, Abraham Lincoln, and Theodore Roosevelt. Washington represents the nation's founding; Jefferson, its philosophy of liberty; Lincoln, its unity; and Roosevelt, its growth.

The monument was the creation of Gutzon Borglum, an immigrant sculptor who designed it and supervised its construction between 1927 and 1941. The name Rushmore comes from Charles E. Rushmore, a New York lawyer who investigated land titles in the Black Hills while searching for a suitable site for the monument. Today, Mount Rushmore is considered one of the wonders of the United States. Each year, it welcomes thousands of visitors from all over the world.

man who, in the concrete pressure of a struggle for national independence by a single people, had the coolness, forecast, and capacity to introduce into a merely revolutionary document an abstract truth, applicable to all men and all times, and so embalm it there that today and in all coming days it

Jefferson wanted to be remembered for three things: the Declaration of Independence, Virginia's law of religious freedom, and the founding of the University of Virginia. These three crowning achievements symbolize his commitment to liberty, tolerance, and knowledge. Yet he is also remembered as a farmer, an inventor, a scientist—and one of America's greatest Presidents. (Library of Congress.)

shall be a rebuke and a stumbling block to the very harbingers of reappearing tyranny and oppression."

Woodrow Wilson honored the scope of Jefferson's intellect when he said, "Jefferson's mind did not move in a world of narrow circumstances; it did not confine itself to the conditions of a single race or a single continent." Wilson added,

"Jefferson's principles are sources of light because they are not made up of pure reason, but spring out of aspiration, impulse, vision, sympathy. They burn with the fervor of the heart; they wear the light of interpretation he sought to speak in, the authentic terms of honest, human ambition."

And in 1962, when John F. Kennedy was the host of a dinner at the White House for a number of Nobel Prize winners, he called the company "the most extraordinary collection of talents, of human knowledge, that has ever gathered together at the White House—with the possible exception of when Thomas Jefferson dined alone."

Revolutionary, farmer, scientist, educator, and President—Thomas Jefferson most surely was, by the standards of his own or any other time, a truly extraordinary man.

Bibliography

Allison, John Murray. *Adams and Jefferson: The Story of a Friendship*. Tulsa: University of Oklahoma Press, 1966. Illustrated with many old pictures and prints, this book tells the story of the long relationship between John Adams and Jefferson, a relationship that alternated between friendship and dislike.

Bottorff, William K. *Thomas Jefferson*. Boston: Twayne, 1979. At 179 pages, this is a compact, readable general account of Jefferson's life and interests.

Bowers, Claude Gernade. *The Young Jefferson*. Boston: Houghton, Mifflin, 1945. Readers interested in Jefferson's early life, his revolutionary activities, and his years in France will enjoy this book, which tells the story of his life up to 1789, the year of his return from France.

Bruns, Roger. *Thomas Jefferson*. New York: Chelsea House Publishers, 1986. Written for younger readers, this 112-page biography is amply illustrated and easy to read.

Dos Passos, John. *The Head and Heart of Thomas Jefferson*. New York: Doubleday, 1954. This study of Jefferson's thinking includes many passages from his essays, letters, and other works.

Falkner, Leonard. *For Thomas Jefferson and Liberty: The United States in War and Peace, 1800–1815*. New York: Knopf, 1972. This 250-page book is aimed at younger readers. It tells the story of Jefferson and his friends, James Madison and James Monroe, during the turbulent early years of the 19th century and the War of 1812.

Gurney, Gene. *Monticello.* New York: Franklin Watts, 1966. Only 74 pages long but crammed with maps and illustrations, this is a colorful, easy-to-read guide for younger readers about one of America's historic showplaces.

Jefferson, Thomas. *A Biography in His Own Words.* By the editors of Newsweek Books, with an introduction by Joseph L. Gardner. New York: Newsweek, distributed by Harper & Row, 1974. More than 400 pages long, this book is Jefferson's life story pieced together from his various writings and many informative footnotes.

Munves, James. *Thomas Jefferson and the Declaration of Independence.* New York: Scribner's, 1978. This 135-page, illustrated account of the writing and editing of the famous Declaration is written for younger readers.

Wilstach, Paul, editor. *The Correspondence of John Adams and Thomas Jefferson, 1812–1826.* New York: Capricorn Books, 1925. Once these two former revolutionaries and Presidents had patched up their quarrel, they delighted in writing long, chatty letters to one another. This collection of their letters gives us a memorable and sometimes funny look into two of the greatest minds of a great age.

Index